WORLD CULTURAL HERITAGE LIBRARY

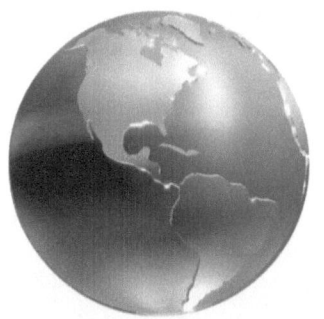

AKBAR, EMPEROR OF INDIA

A PICTURE OF LIFE AND CUSTOMS FROM
THE SIXTEENTH CENTURY
BY
DR. RICHARD VON GARBE

PUBLISHED FIRST: 1909
REPRINT 2014 ISBN: 1-4330-9412-6

AKBAR, EMPEROR OF INDIA
A PICTURE OF LIFE AND CUSTOMS FROM THE SIXTEENTH CENTURY
BY
DR. RICHARD VON GARBE

RECTOR OF THE UNIVERSITY OF TUBINGEN
TRANSLATED FROM THE GERMAN BY LYDIA G.
ROBINSON
Reprinted from "The Monist" of April, 1909
Chicago
The Open Court Publishing Company

1909

AKBAR DIRECTING THE TYING-UP OF A WILD ELEPHANT.
Tempera painting in the Akbar Namahby Abu'l Fazl.
Photographed from the original in the India Museum for The
Place of Animals in Human Thought by the Countess Evelyn
Martinengo Cesaresco.

TABLE OF CONTENTS

LIST OF ILLUSTRATIONS.

Akbar Directing the Tying-up of a Wild Elephant
(*Frontispiece*)
Akbar, Emperor of India
Mausoleum of Akbar's Father, Humâyun
View of Fathpur
Akbar's Grave
Mausoleum of Akbar at Sikandra
The Chakra the Indian Emblem of Empire,

AKBAR, EMPEROR OF INDIA.

The student of India who would at the same time be an historian, discovers to his sorrow that the land of his researches is lamentably poor in historical sources. And if within the realm of historical investigation, a more seductive charm lies for him in the analysis of great personalities than in ascertaining the course of historical development, then verily may he look about in vain for such personalities in the antiquity and middle ages of India. Not that the princely thrones were wanting in great men in ancient India, for we find abundant traces of them in Hindu folk-lore and poetry, but these sources do not extend to establishing the realistic element in details and furnishing life-like portraits of the men themselves. That the Hindu has ever been but little interested in historical matters is a generally recognized fact. Religious and philosophical speculations, dreams of other worlds, of previous and future existences, have claimed the attention of thoughtful minds to a much greater degree than has historical reality.

The misty myth-woven veil which hangs over persons and events of earlier times, vanishes at the beginning of the modern era which in India starts with the Mohammedan conquest, for henceforth the history of India is written by foreigners. Now we meet with men who take a decisive part in the fate of India, and they appear as sharply outlined, even though generally unpleasing, personalities.

Islam has justly been characterized as the caricature of a religion. Fanaticism and fatalism are two conspicuously irreligious emotions, and it is exactly these two emotions, which Islam understands how to arouse in savage peoples, to which it owes the part it has played in the history of the world, and the almost unprecedented success of its diffusion in Asia, Africa and Europe.

About 1000 A.D. India was invaded by the Sultan Mahmud of Ghasna. "With Mahmud's expedition into India begins one of the most horrible periods of the history of Hindustan. One monarch dethrones another, no dynasty continues in power, every accession to the throne is accompanied by the murder of kinsmen, plundering of cities, devastation of the lowlands and the slaughter of thousands of men, women and children of the predecessor's adherents; for five centuries northwest and northern India literally reeked with the blood of multitudes."

[1] Mohammedan dynasties of Afghan, Turkish and Mongolian origin follow that of Ghasna. This entire period is filled with an almost boundless series of battles, intrigues, imbroglios and political revolutions; nearly all events had the one characteristic in common, that they took place amid murder, pillage and fire.

The most frightful spectacle throughout these reeking centuries is the terrible Mongolian prince Timur, a successor of Genghis-Khan, who fell upon India with his band of assassins in the year 1398 and before his entry into Delhi the capital, in which he was proclaimed Emperor of India, caused the hundred thousand prisoners whom he had captured in his previous battles in the Punjab, to be slaughtered in one single day, because it was too inconvenient to drag them around with him.

AKBAR, EMPEROR OF INDIA.

From Noer's Kaiser Akbar, (Frontispiece to Vol. II).

So says Timur himself with shameless frankness in his account of the expedition, and he further relates that after his entry into Delhi, all three districts of the city were plundered "according to the will of God."[2]

In 1526 Baber, a descendant of Timur, made his entry into Delhi and there founded the dominion of the Grand Moguls (i.e., of the great Mongols). The overthrow of this dynasty was brought about by the disastrous reign of Baber's successor Aurungzeb, a cruel, crafty and treacherous despot, who following the example of his ancestor Timur, spread terror and alarm around him in the second half of the seventeenth and the beginning of the eighteenth centuries. Even to-day Hindus may be seen to tremble when they meet the sinister fanatical glance of a Mohammedan.

Princes with sympathetic qualities were not entirely lacking in the seven centuries of Mohammedan dominion in India, and they shine forth as points of light from the gloomy horror of this time, but they fade out completely before the luminous picture of the man who governed India for half a century (1556-1605) and by a wise, gentle and just reign brought about a season of prosperity such as the land had never experienced in the millenniums of its history. This man, whose memory even to-day is revered by the Hindus, was a descendant of Baber, Abul Fath Jelâleddin

Muhammed, known by the surname Akbar "the Great," which was conferred upon the child even when he was named, and completely supplanted the name that properly belonged to him. And truly he justified the epithet, for great, fabulously great, was Akbar as man, general, statesman and ruler,—all in all a prince who deserves to be known by every one whose heart is moved by the spectacle of true human greatness.[3]

When we wish to understand a personality we are in the habit of ascertaining the inherited characteristics, and investigating the influences exercised upon it by religion, family, environment, education, youthful impressions, experience, and so forth. Most men are easily comprehensible as the products of these factors. The more independent of all such influences, or the more in opposition to them, a personality develops, the more attractive and interesting will it appear to us. At the first glance it looks as if the Emperor Akbar had developed his entire character from himself and by his own efforts in total independence of all influences which in other cases are thought to determine the character and nature of a man. A Mohammedan, a Mongol, a descendant of the monster Timur, the son of a weak incapable father, born in exile, called when but a lad to the government of a disintegrated and almost annihilated realm in the India of the sixteenth century,—which means in an age of perfidy, treachery, avarice, and self-seeking,—Akbar appears before us as a noble man, susceptible to all grand and beautiful impressions, conscientious, unprejudiced, and energetic, who knew how to bring peace and order out of the confusion of the times, who throughout his reign desired the furtherance of his subjects' and not of his own interest, who while increasing the privileges of the Mohammedans, not only also declared equality of rights for the Hindus but even actualized that equality, who in every conceivable way sought to conciliate his subjects

so widely at variance with each other in race, customs, and religion, and who finally when the narrow dogmas of his religion no longer satisfied him, attained to a purified faith in God, which was independent of all formulated religions.

A closer observation, however, shows that the contrast is not quite so harsh between what according to our hypotheses Akbar should have been as a result of the forces which build up man, and what he actually became. His predilection for science and art Akbar had inherited from his grandfather Baber and his father Humâyun. His youth, which was passed among dangers and privations, in flight and in prison, was certainly not without a beneficial influence upon Akbar's development into a man of unusual power and energy. And of significance for his spiritual development was the circumstance that after his accession to the throne his guardian put him in the charge of a most excellent tutor, the enlightened and liberal minded Persian Mir Abdullatîf, who laid the foundation for Akbar's later religious and ethical views. Still, however high we may value the influence of this teacher, the main point lay in Akbar's own endowments, his susceptibility for such teaching as never before had struck root with any Mohammedan prince. Akbar had not his equal in the history of Islam. "He is the only prince grown up in the Mohammedan creed whose endeavor it was to ennoble the limitation of this most separatistic of all religions into a true religion of humanity." [4]

Even the external appearance of Akbar appeals to us sympathetically. We sometimes find reproduced a miniature from Delhi which pictures Akbar as seated; in this the characteristic features of the Mongolian race appear softened and refined to a remarkable degree.[B] The shape of the head is rather round, the outlines are softened, the black eyes large, thoughtful, almost dreamy, and only very slightly slanting, the brows full and bushy, the lips somewhat prominent and the nose a tiny bit hooked. The face is beardless except for the rather thin closely cut moustache which falls down over the curve of the month in soft waves. According to the description of his son, the Emperor Jehângir, Akbar's complexion is said to have been the yellow of wheat; the Portuguese Jesuits who came to his court called it plainly white. Although not exactly beautiful, Akbar seemed beautiful to many of his contemporaries, including Europeans, probably because of the august and at the same time kind and winsome expression which his countenance bore. Akbar was rather tall, broad-shouldered, strongly built and had long arms and hands.

Akbar, the son of the dethroned Emperor Humâyun, was born on October 14, 1542, at Amarkot in Sindh, two years after his father had been deprived of his kingdom by the usurper Shêr Chân. After an exile of fifteen years, or rather after an aimless wandering and flight of that length, the indolent pleasure-and opium-loving Humâyun was again permitted to return to his capital in 1555,—not through his own merit but that of his energetic general Bairâm Chân, a Turk who in one decisive battle had overcome the Afghans, at that time in possession of the dominion. But Humâyun was not long to enjoy his regained throne; half a year later he fell down a stairway in his palace and died. In January 1556 Akbar, then thirteen years of age, ascended the throne. Because of his youthful years Bairâm Chân assumed the regency as guardian of the realm or "prince-father" as it is expressed in Hindî, and guided the wavering ship of state with a strong hand. He overthrew various insurgents and disposed of them with cold cruelty. But after a few years he so aroused the illwill of Akbar by deeds of partiality, selfishness and violence that in March 1560 Akbar, then 17 years of age, decided to take the reins of government into his own hand. Deprived of his office and influence Bairâm Chân hastened to the Punjab and took arms against his Imperial Master. Akbar led his troops in person against the rebel and overcame him. When barefooted, his turban thrown around his neck, Bairâm Chân appeared before Akbar and prostrated himself before the throne, Akbar did not do the thing which was customary under such circumstances in the Orient in all ages. The magnanimous youth did not sentence the humiliated rebel to a painful death but bade him arise in memory of the great services which Bairâm Chân had rendered to his father and later to himself, and again assume his old place of honor at the right of the throne. Before the assembled nobility he gave him the choice whether he would take the governorship of a province, or would enjoy the favor of his master at court as a benefactor of the imperial family, or whether, accompanied by an escort befitting his rank, he would prefer to undertake a pilgrimage to Mecca.[5] Bairâm Chân was wise enough to choose the last, but on the way to Mecca he was killed by an Afghan and the news caused Akbar sincere grief and led him to take the four year old son of Bairâm Chân under his special protection.

Mâhum Anâga, the Emperor's nurse, for whom he felt a warm attachment and gratitude, a woman revengeful and ambitious but loyal and devoted to Akbar, had contributed in bringing about the fall of the regent. She had cared for the Emperor from his birth to his accession and amid the confusion of his youth had guarded him from danger; but for this service she expected her reward. She sought nothing less than in the rôle of an intimate confidante of the youthful Emperor to be secretly the actual ruler of India.

Mâhum Anâga had a son, Adham Chân by name, to whom at her suggestion Akbar assigned the task of reconquering and governing the province of Mâlwâ. Adham Chân was a passionate and violent man, as ambitious and avaricious as his mother, and behaved himself in Mâlwâ as if he were an independent prince. As soon as Akbar learned this he advanced by forced marches to Mâlwâ and surprised his disconcerted foster-brother before the latter could be warned by his mother. But Adham Chân had no difficulty in obtaining Akbar's forgiveness for his infringements.

On the way back to Agra, where the Emperor at that time was holding court, a noteworthy incident happened. Akbar had ridden alone in advance of his escort and suddenly found himself face to face with a powerful tigress who with her five cubs came out from the shrubbery across his path. His approaching attendants found the nineteen year old

Emperor standing quietly by the side of the slaughtered beast which he had struck to the ground with a single blow of his sword. To how much bodily strength, intrepidity, cold-blooded courage and sure-sightedness this blow of the sword testified which dared not come the fraction of a second too late, may be judged by every one who has any conception of the spring of a raging tigress anxious for the welfare of her young. And we may easily surmise the thoughts which the sight aroused in the minds of the Mohammedan nobles in Akbar's train. At that moment many ambitious wishes and designs may have been carried to their grave.[6]

The Emperor soon summoned his hot-headed foster-brother Adham Chân to court in order to keep him well in sight for he had counted often enough on Akbar's affection for his mother Mâhum Anâga to save him from the consequences of his sins. Now Mâhum Anâga, her son and her adherents, hated the grand vizier with a deadly hatred because they perceived that they were being deprived of their former influence in matters of state. This hatred finally impelled Adham Chân to a senseless undertaking. The embittered man hatched up a conspiracy against the grand vizier and when one night in the year 1562 the latter was attending a meeting of political dignitaries on affairs of state in the audience hall of the Imperial palace, Adham Chân with his conspirators suddenly broke in and stabbed the grand vizier in the breast, whereupon his companions slew the wounded man with their swords. Even now the deluded Adham Chân counted still upon the Emperor's forbearance and upon the influence of his mother. Akbar was aroused by the noise and leaving his apartments learned what had happened. Adham Chân rushed to the Emperor, seized his arm and begged him to listen to his explanations. But the Emperor was beside himself with rage, struck the murderer with his fist so that he fell to the floor and commanded the terrified servants to bind him with fetters and throw him head over heels from the terrace of the palace to the courtyard below. The horrible deed was done but the wretch was not dead. Then the Emperor commanded the shattered body of the dying man to be dragged up the stairs again by the hair and to be flung once more to the ground.[7]

I have related this horrible incident in order to give Akbar's picture with the utmost possible faithfulness and without idealization. Akbar was a rough, strong-nerved man, who was seldom angry but whose wrath when once aroused was fearful. It is a blemish on his character that in some cases he permitted himself to be carried away to such cruel death sentences, but we must not forget that he was then dealing with the punishment of particularly desperate criminals, and that such severe judgments had always been considered in the Orient to be righteous and sensible. Not only in the Orient unfortunately,—even in Europe 200 years after Akbar's time tortures and the rack were applied at the behest of courts of law.

Mahum Anâga came too late to save her son. Akbar sought with tender care to console her for his dreadful end but the heart-broken woman survived the fearful blow of fate only about forty days. The Emperor caused her body to be buried with that of her son in one common grave at Delhi, and he himself accompanied the funeral procession. At his command a stately monument was erected above this grave which still stands to-day. His generosity and clemency were also shown in the fact that he extended complete pardon to the accomplices in the murder of the grand vizier and even permitted them to retain their offices and dignities because he was convinced that they had been drawn into the crime by the violent Adham Chân. In other ways too Akbar showed himself to be ready to grant pardon to an almost incomprehensible extent. Again and again when an insubordinate viceroy in the provinces would surrender after an unsuccessful uprising Akbar would let him off without any penalty, thus giving him the opportunity of revolting again after a short time.

It was an eventful time in which Akbar arrived at manhood in the midst of all sorts of personal dangers.

MAUSOLEUM OF AKBAR'S FATHER, HUMÂYUN.

MAUSOLEUM OF AKBAR'S FATHER, HUMÂYUN.

I will pass over with but few comments his military expeditions which can have no interest for the general public. When Akbar ascended the throne his realm comprised only a very small portion of the possessions which had been subject to his predecessors. With the energy which was a fundamental characteristic of his nature he once more took possession of the provinces which had been torn from the empire, at the same time undertaking the conquest of new lands, and accomplished this task with such good fortune that in the fortieth year of his reign the empire of India covered more territory than ever before; that is to say, not only the whole of Hindustan including the peninsula Gujerat, the lands of the Indus and

Kashmir but also Afghanistan and a larger part of the Dekkhan than had ever been subject to any former Padishah of Delhi. At this time while the Emperor had his residence at Lahore the phrase was current in India, "As lucky as Akbar."[8]

It was apparent often enough in the military expeditions that Akbar far surpassed his contemporaries in generalship. But it was not the love of war and conquest which drove him each time anew to battle; a sincere desire inspired by a mystical spirit impelled him to bring to an end the ceaseless strife between the small states of India by joining them to his realm, and thus to found a great united empire.[9]

More worthy of admiration than the subjugation of such large territories in which of course many others have also been successful, is the fact that Akbar succeeded in establishing order, peace, and prosperity in the regained and newly subjugated provinces. This he brought about by the introduction of a model administration, an excellent police, a regulated post service, and especially a just division of taxes.[10] Up to Akbar's time corruption had been a matter of course in the entire official service and enormous sums in the treasury were lost by peculation on the part of tax collectors.

Akbar first divided the whole realm into twelve and later into fifteen viceregencies, and these into provinces, administrative districts and lesser subdivisions, and governed the revenues of the empire on the basis of a uniformly exact survey of the land. He introduced a standard of measurement, replacing the hitherto customary land measure (a leather strap which was easily lengthened or shortened according to the need of the measuring officer) by a new instrument of measurement in the form of a bamboo staff which was provided with iron rings at definite intervals. For purposes of assessment land was divided into four classes according to the kind of cultivation practiced upon it. The first class comprised arable land with a constant rotation of crops; the second, that which had to lie fallow for from one to two years in order to be productive; the third from three to four years; the fourth that land which was uncultivated for five years and longer or was not arable at all. The first two classes of acreage were taxed one-third of the crop, which according to our present ideas seems an exorbitantly high rate, and it was left to the one assessed whether he would pay the tax in kind or in cash. Only in the case of luxuries or manufactured articles, that is to say, where the use of a circulating medium could be assumed, was cash payment required. Whoever cultivated unreclaimed land was assisted by the government by the grant of a free supply of seed and by a considerable reduction in his taxes for the first four years.

Akbar also introduced a new uniform standard of coinage, but stipulated that the older coins which were still current should be accepted from peasants for their full face value. From all this the Indian peasants could see that Emperor Akbar not only desired strict justice to rule but also wished to further their interests, and the peasants had always comprised the greatest part of the inhabitants, (even according to the latest census in 1903, vol. I, p. 3, 50 to 84 percent of the inhabitants of India live by agriculture). But Akbar succeeded best in winning the hearts

of the native inhabitants by lifting the hated poll tax which still existed side by side with all other taxes.

The founder of Islam had given the philanthropical command to exterminate from the face of the earth all followers of other faiths who were not converted to Islam, but he had already convinced himself that it was impossible to execute this law. And, indeed, if the Mohammedans had followed out this precept, how would they have been able to overthrow land upon land and finally even thickly populated India where the so-called unbelievers comprised an overwhelming majority? Therefore in place of complete extermination the more practical arrangement of the poll tax was instituted, and this was to be paid by all unbelievers in order to be a constant reminder to them of the loss of their independence. This humiliating burden which was still executed in the strictest, most inconsiderate manner, Akbar removed in the year 1565 without regard to the very considerable loss to the state's treasury. Nine years later followed the removal of the tax upon religious assemblies and pilgrimages, the execution of which had likewise kept the Hindus in constant bitterness towards their Mohammedan rulers.

Sometime previous to these reforms Akbar had abolished a custom so disgusting that we can hardly comprehend that it ever could have legally existed. At any rate it alone is sufficient to brand Islam and its supreme contempt for followers of other faiths, with one of the greatest stains in the history of humanity. When a tax-collector gathered the taxes of the Hindus and the payment had been made, the Hindu was required "without the slightest sign of fear of defilement" to open his mouth in order that the tax collector might spit in it if he wished to do so.

[11] This was much more than a disgusting humiliation. When the tax-collector availed himself of this privilege the Hindu lost thereby his greatest possession, his caste, and was shut out from any intercourse with his equals. Accordingly he was compelled to pass his whole life trembling in terror before this horrible evil which threatened him. That a man of Akbar's nobility of character should remove such an atrocious, yes devilish, decree seems to

us a matter of course; but for the Hindus it was an enormous beneficence.

Akbar sought also to advance trade and commerce in every possible way. He regulated the harbor and toll duties, removed the oppressive taxes on cattle, trees, grain and other produce as well as the customary fees of subjects at every possible appointment or office. In the year 1574 it was decreed that the loss which agriculture suffered by the passage of royal troops through the fields should be carefully calculated and scrupulously replaced.

Besides these practical regulations for the advancement of the material welfare, Akbar's efforts for the ethical uplift of his subjects are noteworthy. Drunkenness and debauchery were punished and he sought to restrain prostitution by confining dancing girls and abandoned women in one quarter set apart for them outside of his residence which received the name *Shâitânpura* or "Devil's City." [12]

The existing corruption in the finance and customs department was abolished by means of a complicated and punctilious system of supervision (the bureaus of receipts and expenditures were kept entirely separated from each other in the treasury department,) and Akbar himself carefully examined the accounts handed in each month from every district, just as he gave his personal attention with tireless industry and painstaking care to every detail in the widely ramified domain of the administration of government. Moreover the Emperor was fortunate in having at the head of the finance department a prudent, energetic, perfectly honorable and incorruptible man, the Hindu Todar Mal, who without possessing the title of vizier or minister of state had assumed all the functions of such an office.

It is easily understood that many of the higher tax officials did not grasp the sudden break of a new day but continued to oppress and impoverish the peasants in the traditional way, but the system established by Akbar succeeded admirably and soon brought all such transgressions to light. Todar Mal held a firm rein, and by throwing hundreds of these faithless officers into prison and by making ample use of bastinado and torture, spread abroad such a wholesome terror that Akbar's reforms were soon victorious.

How essential it was to exercise the strictest control over men occupying the highest positions may be seen by the example of the feudal nobility whose members bore the title "Jâgîrdâr." Such a Jâgîrdâr had to provide a contingent of men and horses for the imperial army corresponding to the size of the estate which was given him in fief. Now it had been a universal custom for the Jâgîrdârs to provide themselves with fewer soldiers and horses on a military expedition than at the regular muster. Then too the men and horses often proved useless for severe service. When the reserves were mustered the knights dressed up harmless private citizens as soldiers or hired them for the occasion and after the muster was over, let them go again. In the same way the horses brought forward for the muster were taken back into private service immediately afterwards and were replaced by worthless animals for the imperial service. This evil too was abolished at one stroke, by taking an exact personal description of the soldiers presented and by branding the heads of horses, elephants and camels with certain marks. By this simple expedient it became impossible to exchange men and animals presented

at the muster for worthless material and also to loan them to other knights during muster.

The number of men able to bear arms in Akbar's realm has been given as about four and a half millions but the standing army which was held at the expense of the state was small in proportion. It contained only about twenty-five thousand men, one-half of whom comprised the cavalry and the rest musketry and artillery; Since India does not produce first class horses, Akbar at once provided for the importation of noble steeds from other lands of the Orient which were famed for horse breeding and was accustomed to pay more for such animals than the price which was demanded. In the same way no expense was too great for him to spend on the breeding and nurture of elephants, for they were very valuable animals for the warfare of that day. His stables contained from five to six thousand well-trained elephants. The breeding of camels and mules he also advanced with a practical foresight and understood how to overcome the widespread prejudice in India against the use of mules.

Untiringly did Akbar inspect stables, arsenals, military armories, and shipyards, and insisted on perfect order in all departments. He called the encouragement of seamanship an act of worship

[13] but was not able to make India, a maritime power.

Akbar had an especial interest in artillery, and with it a particular gift for the technique and great skill in mechanical matters. He invented a cannon which could be taken apart to be carried more easily on the march and could be put up quickly, apparently for use in mountain batteries. By another invention he united seventeen cannons in such a way that they could be shot off simultaneously by one fuse.[14] Hence it is probably a sort of *mitrailleuse*. Akbar is also said to have invented a mill cart which served as a mill as well as for carrying freight. With regard to these inventions we must take into consideration the possibility that the real inventor may have been some one else, but that the flatterers at the court ascribed them to the Emperor because the initiative may have originated with him.

(II, 372) because of the so-called "organ cannons" which were in use in Europe as early as the 15th century.

The details which I have given will suffice to show what perfection the military and civil administration attained through Akbar's efforts. Throughout his empire order and justice reigned and a prosperity hitherto unknown. Although taxes were never less oppressive in India than under Akbar's reign, the imperial income for one year amounted to more than $120,000,000, a sum at which contemporary Europe marveled, and which we must consider in the light of the much greater purchasing power of money in the sixteenth century.

[15] A large part of Akbar's income was used in the erection of benevolent institutions, of inns along country roads in which travelers were entertained at the imperial expense, in the support of the poor, in gifts for pilgrims, in granting loans whose payment was never demanded, and many similar ways. To his encouragement of schools, of literature, art and science I will refer later.

Of decided significance for Akbar's success was his patronage of the native population. He did not limit his efforts to lightening the lot of the subjugated Hindus and relieving them of oppressive burdens; his efforts went deeper. He wished to educate the Mohammedans and Hindus to a feeling of mutual good-will and confidence, and in doing so he was obliged to contend in the one case against haughtiness and inordinate ambition, and in the other against hate and distrustful reserve. If with this end in view he actually favored the Hindus by keeping certain ones close to him and advancing them to the most influential positions in the state, he did it because he found characteristics in the Hindus (especially in their noblest race, the Rajputs) which seemed to him most valuable for the stability of the empire and for the promotion of the general welfare. He had seen enough faithlessness in the Mohammedan nobles and in his own relatives. Besides, Akbar was born in the house of a small Rajput prince who had shown hospitality to Akbar's parents on their flight and had given them his protection.

The Rajputs are the descendants of the ancient Indian warrior race and are a brave, chivalrous, trustworthy people who possess a love of freedom and pride of race quite different in character from the rest of the Hindus. Even to-day every traveler in India thinks he has been set down in another world when he treads the ground of Rajputâna and sees around him in place of the weak effeminate servile inhabitants of other parts of the country powerful upright men, splendid warlike figures with blazing defiant eyes and long waving beards.

While Akbar valued the Rajputs very highly his own personality was entirely fitted to please these proud manly warriors. An incident which took place before the end of the first year of Akbar's reign is characteristic of the relations which existed on the basis of this intrinsic relationship.[16]

VIEW OF FATHPUR

Bihâri Mal was a prince of the small Rajput state Ambir, and possessed sufficient political comprehension to understand after Akbar's first great successes that his own insignificant power and the nearness of Delhi made it advisable to voluntarily recognize the Emperor as his liege lord. Therefore he came with son, grandson and retainers to swear allegiance to Akbar. Upon his arrival at the imperial camp before Delhi, a most surprising sight met his eyes. Men were running in every direction, fleeing wildly before a raging elephant who wrought destruction to everything that came within his reach. Upon the neck of this enraged brute sat a young man in perfect calmness belaboring the animal's head with the iron prong which is used universally in India for guiding elephants. The Rajputs sprang from their horses and came up perfectly unconcerned to observe the interesting spectacle, and broke out in loud applause when the conquered elephant knelt down in exhaustion. The young man sprang from its back and cordially greeted the Rajput princes (who now for the first time recognized Akbar in the elephant-tamer) bidding them welcome to his red imperial tent. From this occurrence dates the friendship of the two men. In later years Bihâri Mai's son and grandson occupied high places in the imperial service, and Akbar married a daughter of the Rajput chief who became the mother of his son and successor Selim, afterwards the Emperor Jehângir. Later on Akbar received a number of other Rajput women in his harem.

Not all of Akbar's relations to the Rajputs however were of such a friendly kind. As his grandfather Baber before him, he had many bitter battles with them, for no other Indian people had opposed him so vigorously as they. Their domain blocked the way to the south, and from their rugged mountains and strongly fortified cities the Rajputs harassed the surrounding country by many invasions and destroyed order, commerce and communication quite after the manner of the German robber barons of the Middle Ages. Their overthrow was accordingly a public necessity.

The most powerful of these Rajput chiefs was the Prince of Mewâr who had particularly attracted the attention of the Emperor by his support of the rebels. The

control of Mewâr rested upon the possession of the fortress Chitor which was built on a monstrous cliff one hundred and twenty meters high, rising abruptly from the plain and was equipped with every means of defence that could be contrived by the military skill of that time for an incomparably strong bulwark. On the plain at its summit which measured over twelve kilometers in circumference a city well supplied with water lay within the fortification walls. There an experienced general, Jaymal, "the Lion of Chitor," was in command. I have not time to relate the particulars of the siege, the laying of ditches and mines and the uninterrupted battles which preceded the fall of Chitor in February, 1568. According to Akbar's usual custom he exposed himself to showers of bullets without once being hit (the superstition of his soldiers considered him invulnerable) and finally the critical shot was one in which Akbar with his own hand laid low the brave commander of Chitor. Then the defenders considered their cause lost, and the next night saw a barbarous sight, peculiarly Indian in character: the so-called Jauhar demanded his offering according to an old Rajput custom. Many great fires gleamed weirdly in the fortress. To escape imprisonment and to save their honor from the horrors of captivity, the women mounted the solemnly arranged funeral pyres, while all the men, clad in saffron hued garments, consecrated themselves to death. When the victors entered the city on the next morning a battle began which raged until the third evening, when there was no one left to kill. Eight thousand warriors had fallen, besides thirty thousand inhabitants of Chitor who had participated in the fight.

With the conquest of Chitor which I have treated at considerable length because it ended in a typically Indian manner, the resistance of the Rajputs broke down. After Akbar had attained his purpose he was on the friendliest

terms with the vanquished. It testifies to his nobility of character as well as to his political wisdom that after this complete success he not only did not celebrate a triumph, but on the contrary proclaimed the renown of the vanquished throughout all India by erecting before the gate of the imperial palace at Delhi two immense stone elephants with the statues of Jaymal, the "Lion of Chitor," and of the noble youth Pata who had performed the most heroic deeds in the defense of Chitor. By thus honoring his conquered foes in such a magnanimous manner Akbar found the right way to the heart of the Rajputs. By constant bestowal of favors he gradually succeeded in so reconciling the noble Rajputs to the loss of their independence that they were finally glad and proud to devote themselves to his service, and, under the leadership of their own princes, proved themselves to be the best and truest soldiers of the imperial army, even far from their home in the farthest limits of the realm.

The great masses of the Hindu people Akbar won over by lowering the taxes as we have previously related, and by all the other successful expedients for the prosperity of the country, but especially by the concession of perfect liberty of faith and worship and by the benevolent interest with which he regarded the religious practices of the Hindus. A people in whom religion is the ruling motive of life, after enduring all the dreadful sufferings of previous centuries for its religion's sake, must have been brought to a state; of boundless reverence by Akbar's attitude. And since the Hindus were accustomed to look upon the great heroes and benefactors of humanity as incarnations of deity we shall not be surprised to read from an author of that time

[17] that every morning before sunrise great numbers of Hindus crowded together in front of the palace to await the appearance of Akbar and to prostrate themselves as soon as he was seen at a window, at the same time singing religious hymns. This fanatical enthusiasm of the Hindus

for his person Akbar knew how to retain not only by actual benefits but also by small, well calculated devices.

It is a familiar fact that the Hindus considered the Ganges to be a holy river and that cows were sacred animals. Accordingly we can easily understand Akbar's purpose when we learn that at every meal he drank regularly of water from the Ganges (carefully filtered and purified to be sure) calling it "the water of immortality,"

[18] and that later he forbade the slaughtering of cattle and eating their flesh.[19] But Akbar did not go so far in his connivance with the Hindus that he considered all their customs good or took them under his protection. For instance he forbade child marriages among the Hindus, that is to say the marriage of boys under sixteen and of girls under fourteen years, and he permitted the remarriage of widows. The barbaric customs of Brahmanism were repugnant to his very soul. He therefore most strictly forbade the slaughtering of animals for purposes of sacrifice, the use of ordeals for the execution of justice, and the burning of widows against their will, which indeed was not established according to Brahman law but was constantly practiced according to traditional custom.[20] To be sure neither Akbar nor his successor Jehângir were permanently successful in their efforts to put an end to the burning of widows. Not until the year 1829 was the horrible

custom practically done away with through the efforts of the English.

Throughout his entire life Akbar was a tirelessly industrious, restlessly active man. By means of ceaseless activity he struggled successfully against his natural tendency to melancholy and in this way kept his mind wholesome, which is most deserving of admiration in an Oriental monarch who was brought in contact day by day with immoderate flattery and idolatrous veneration. Well did Akbar know that no Oriental nation can be governed without a display of dazzling splendor; but in the midst of the fabulous luxury with which Akbar's court was fitted out and his camp on the march, in the possession of an incomparably rich harem which accompanied the Emperor on his expeditions and journeys in large palatial tents, Akbar always showed a remarkable moderation. It is true that he abolished the prohibition of wine which Islam had inaugurated and had a court cellar in his palace, but he himself drank only a little wine and only ate once a day and then did not fully satisfy his hunger at this one meal which he ate alone and not at any definite time.[21] Though he was not strictly a vegetarian yet he lived mainly on rice, milk, fruits and sweets, and meat was repulsive to him. He is said to have eaten meat hardly more than four times a year.[22]

Akbar was very fond of flowers and perfumes and especially enjoyed blooded doves whose care he well understood. About twenty thousand of these peaceful birds are said to have made their home on the battlements of his palace. His historian[23] relates: "His Majesty deigned to improve them in a marvelous manner by crossing the races which had not been done formerly."

Akbar was passionately fond of hunting and pursued the noble sport in its different forms, especially the tiger hunt and the trapping of wild elephants,[24] but he also hunted with trained falcons and leopards, owning no less than nine hundred hunting leopards. He was not fond of battue; he enjoyed the excitement and exertion of theactual hunt as a means for exercise and recreation, for training the eye and quickening the blood. Akbar took pleasure also in games. Besides chess, cards and other games, fights between animals may especially be mentioned, of which elephant fights were the most common, but there were also contests between camels, buffaloes, cocks, and even frogs, sparrows and spiders.

Usually, however, the whole day was filled up from the first break of dawn for Akbar with affairs of government and audiences, for every one who had a request or a grievance to bring forward could have access to Akbar, and he showed the same interest in the smallest incidents as in the greatest affairs of state. He also held courts of justice wherever he happened to be residing. No criminal could be punished there without his knowledge and no sentence of death executed until Akbar had given the command three times.

[25]

Not until after sunset did the Emperor's time of recreation begin. Since he only required three hours of sleep[26] he devoted most of the night to literary, artistic and scientific occupations. Especially poetry and music delighted his heart. He collected a large library in his palace and drew the most famous scholars and poets to his court. The most important of these were the brothers Abul Faiz (with the *nom de plume* Faizî) and Abul Fazl who have made Akbar's fame known to the whole world through their works. The former at Akbar's behest translated a series of Sanskrit works into Persian, and Abul Fazl, the highly gifted minister and historian of Akbar's court (who to be sure can not be exonerated from the charge of flattery) likewise composed in the Persian language a large historical work written in the most flowery style which is the main source of our knowledge of that period. This famous work is divided in two parts, the first one of which under the title *Akbarnâme*, "Akbar Book," contains the complete history of Akbar's reign, whereas the second part, the *Aîn î Akbarî*, "The Institutions of Akbar," gives a presentation of the political and religious constitution and administration of

India under Akbar's reign. It is also deserving of mention in this connection that Akbar instituted a board for contemporary chronicles, whose duty it was to compose the official record of all events relating to the Emperor and the government as well as to collect all laws and decrees.[27]

When Akbar's recreation hours had come in the night the poets of his court brought their verses. Translations of famous works in Sanskrit literature, of the New Testament and of other interesting books were read aloud, all of which captivated the vivacious mind of the Emperor from which nothing was farther removed than onesidedness and narrow-mindedness. Akbar had also a discriminating appreciation for art and industries. He himself designed the plans for some extremely beautiful candelabra, and the manufacture of tapestry reached such a state of perfection in India under his personal supervision that in those days fabrics were produced in the great imperial factories which in beauty and value excelled the famous rugs of Persia. With still more important results Akbar influenced the realm of architecture in that he discovered how to combine two completely different styles. For indeed, the union of Mohammedan and Indian motives in the buildings of Akbar (who here as in all other departments strove to perfect the complete elevation of national and religious details) to form an improved third style,[28] is entirely original.

Among other ways Akbar betrayed the scientific trend of his mind by sending out an expedition in search of the sources of the Ganges.[29]That a man of such a wonderful degree of versatility should have recognized the value of general education and have devoted himself to its improvement, we would simply take for granted. Akbar caused schools to be erected throughout his whole kingdom for the children of Hindus and Mohammedans, whereas he himself did not know how to read or write.[30] This remarkable fact would seem incredible to us after considering all the above mentioned facts if it was not confirmed by the express testimony of his son, the Emperor Jehângir. At any rate for an illiterate man Akbar certainly accomplished an astonishing amount. The universal character of the endowments of this man could not have been increased by the learning of the schools.

I have now come to the point which arouses most strongly the universal human interest in Akbar, namely, to his religious development and his relation to the religions, or better to religion.

AKBAR'S GRAVE.

AKBAR'S GRAVE.

But first I must protest against the position maintained by a competent scholar[31]that Akbar himself was just as indifferent to religious matters as was the house of Timur as a whole. Against this view we have the testimony of the conscientiousness with which he daily performed his morning and evening devotions, the value which he placed upon fasting and prayer as a means of self-discipline, and the regularity with which he made yearly pilgrimages to the graves of Mohammedan saints.

A better insight into Akbar's heart than these regular observances of worship which might easily be explained by the force of custom is given by the extraordinary manifestations of a devout disposition. When we learn that Akbar invariably prayed at the grave of his father in Delhi[32]before starting upon any important undertaking, or that during the siege of Chitor he made a vow to make a pilgrimage to a shrine in Ajmir after the fall of the fortress, and that after Chitor was in his power he performed this journey in the simplest pilgrim garb, tramping barefooted over the glowing sand,[33] it is impossible for us to look upon Akbar as irreligious. On the contrary nothing moved the Emperor so strongly and insistently as the striving after religious truth. This effort led to a struggle against the most destructive power in his kingdom, against the Mohammedan priesthood. That Akbar, the conqueror in all domains, should also have been victorious in the struggle against the encroachments of the Church (the bitterest struggle which a ruler can undertake), this alone should insure him a place among the greatest of humanity.

The Mohammedan priesthood, the community of the Ulemâs in whose hands lay also the execution of justice according to the dictates of Islam, had attained great prosperity in India by countless large bequests. Its distinguished membership formed an influential party at court. This party naturally represented the Islam of the stricter observance, the so-called Sunnitic Islam, and displayed the greatest severity and intolerance towards the representatives of every more liberal interpretation and towards unbelievers. The chief judge of Agra sentenced men to death because they were Shiites, that is to say they belonged to the other branch of Islam, and the Ulemâs urged Akbar to proceed likewise against the heretics.[34] That arrogance and vanity, selfishness and avarice, also belonged to the character of the Ulemâs is so plainly to be taken for granted according to all analogies that it need hardly be mentioned. The judicature was everywhere utilized by the Ulemâs as a means for illegitimate enrichment.

This ecclesiastical party which in its narrow-minded folly considered itself in possession of the whole truth, stands opposed to the noble skeptic Akbar, whose doubt of the divine origin of the Koran and of the truth of its dogmas began so to torment him that he would pass entire nights sitting out of doors on a stone lost in contemplation. The above mentioned brothers Faizî and Abul Fazl introduced to his impressionable spirit the exalted teaching of Sûfism, the Mohammedan mysticism whose spiritual pantheism had its origin in, or at least was strongly influenced by, the doctrine of the All-One, held by the Brahman Vedânta system. The Sûfi doctrine teaches religious tolerance and has apparently strengthened Akbar in his repugnance towards the intolerant exclusiveness of Sunnitic Islam.

The Ulemâs must have been horror-stricken when they found out that Akbar even sought religious instruction from the hated Brahmans. We hear especially of two, Purushottama and Debî by name, the first of whom taught Sanskrit and Brahman philosophy to the Emperor in his palace, whereas the second was drawn up on a platform to the wall of the palace in the dead of the night and there, suspended in midair, gave lessons on profound esoteric doctrines of the Upanishads to the emperor as he sat by the window. A characteristic bit of Indian local color! The proud Padishah of India, one of the most powerful rulers of his time, listening in the silence of night to the words of the Brahman suspended there outside, who himself as proud as the Emperor would not set foot inside the dwelling of one who in his eyes was unclean, but who would not refuse his wisdom to a sincere seeker after truth.

Akbar left no means untried to broaden his religious outlook. From Gujerat he summoned some Parsees, followers of the religion of Zarathustra, and through them informed himself of their faith and their highly developed

system of ethics which places the sinful thought on the same level with the sinful word and act.

From olden times the inhabitants of India have had a predisposition for religious and philosophical disputations. So Akbar, too, was convinced of the utility of free discussion on religious dogmas. Based upon this idea, and perhaps also in the hope that the Ulemâs would be discomfited Akbar founded at Fathpur Sikrî, his favorite residence in the vicinity of Agra, the famous Ibâdat Khâna, literally the "house of worship," but in reality the house of controversy. This was a splendid structure composed of four halls in which scholars and religious men of all sects gathered together every Thursday evening and were given an opportunity to defend their creeds in the presence and with the cooperation of the Emperor. Akbar placed the discussion in charge of the wise and liberal minded Abul Fazl. How badly the Ulemâs, the representatives of Mohammedan orthodoxy, came off on these controversial evenings was to be foreseen. Since they had no success with their futile arguments they soon resorted to cries of fury, insults for their opponents and even to personal violence, often turning against each other and hurling curses upon their own number. In these discussions the inferiority of the Ulemâs, who nevertheless had always put forth such great claims, was so plainly betrayed that Akbar learned to have a profound contempt for them.

In addition to this, the fraud and machinations by means of which the Ulemâs had unlawfully enriched themselves became known to the Emperor. At any rate there was sufficient ground for the chastisement which Akbar now visited upon the high clergy. In the year 1579 a decree was issued which assigned to the Emperor the final decision in matters of faith, and this was subscribed to by the chiefs of the Ulemâs,—with what personal feelings we can well imagine. For by this act the Ulemâs were deprived of

their ecclesiastical authority which was transferred to the Emperor. That the Orient too possesses its particular official manner of expression in administrative matters is very prettily shown by a decree in which Akbar "granted the long cherished wish" of these same chiefs of the Ulemâs to undertake the pilgrimage to Mecca, which of course really meant a banishment of several years. Other unworthy Ulemâs were displaced from their positions or deprived of their sinecures; others who in their bitterness had caused rebellion or incited or supported mutiny were condemned for high treason. The rich property of the churches was for the most part confiscated and appropriated for the general weal. In short, the power and influence of the Ulemâs was completely broken down, the mosques stood empty and were transformed into stables and warehouses.

Akbar had long ceased to be a faithful Moslem. Now after the fall of the Ulemâs he came forward openly with his conviction, declared the Koran to be a human compilation and its commands folly, disputed the miracles of Mohammed and also the value of his prophecies, and denied the doctrine of recompense after death. He professed the Brahman and Sûfistic doctrine that the soul migrates through countless existences and finally attains divinity after complete purification.

The assertion of the Ulemâs that every person came into the world predisposed towards Islam and that the natural language of mankind was Arabic (the Jews made the same claim for Hebrew and the Brahmans for Sanskrit), Akbar refuted by a drastic experiment which does not correspond with his usual benevolence, but still is characteristic of the tendency of his mind. In this case a convincing demonstration appeared to him so necessary that some individuals would have to suffer for it. Accordingly in the year 1579 he caused twenty infants to be

taken from their parents in return for a compensation and brought up under the care of silent nurses in a remote spot in which no word should be spoken. After four years it was proved that as many of these unhappy children as were still alive were entirely dumb and possessed no trace of a predisposition for Islam.[35] Later the children are said to have learned to speak with extraordinary difficulty as was to be expected.

Akbar's repugnance to Islam developed into a complete revulsion against every thing connected with this narrow religion and made the great Emperor petty-souled in this particular. The decrees were dated from the death of Mohammed and no longer from the Hejra (the flight from Mecca to Medina). Books written in Arabic, the language of the Koran were given the lowest place in the imperial library. The knowledge of Arabic was prohibited, even the sounds characteristically belonging to this language were avoided.[36] Where formerly according to ancient tradition had stood the word *Bismilâhi*, "in the name of God," there now appeared the old war cry *Allâhu akbar* "God is great," which came into use the more generally—on coins, documents, etc.—the more the courtiers came to reverse the sense of the slogan and to apply to it the meaning, "Akbar is God."

Before I enter into the Emperor's assumption of this flattery and his conception of the imperial dignity as conferred by the grace of God, I must speak of the interesting attempts of the Jesuits to win over to Christianity the most powerful ruler of the Orient.

As early as in the spring of 1578 a Portuguese Jesuit who worked among the Bengals as a missionary appeared at the imperial court and pleased Akbar especially because he got the better of the Ulemâs in controversy. Two years later Akbar sent a very polite letter to the Provincial of the Jesuit order in Goa, requesting him to send two Fathers in order that Akbar himself might be instructed "in their faith and its perfection." It is easy to imagine how gladly the Provincial assented to this demand and how carefully he proceeded with the selection of the fathers who were to be sent away with such great expectations. As gifts to the Emperor the Jesuits brought a Bible in four languages and pictures of Christ and the Virgin Mary, and to their great delight when Akbar received them he laid the Bible upon his head and kissed the two pictures as a sign of reverence.

[37]

In the interesting work of the French Jesuit Du Jarric, published in 1611, we possess very detailed accounts of the operations of these missionaries who were honorably received at Akbar's court and who were invited to take up their residence in the imperial palace. The evening assemblies in the 'Ibâdat Khâna' in Fathpur Sikrî at once gave the shrewd Jesuits who were schooled in dialectics, an opportunity to distinguish themselves before the Emperor who himself presided over this Religious

Parliament in which Christians, Jews, Mohammedans, Brahmans, Buddhists and Parsees debated with each other. Abul Fazl speaks with enthusiasm in the *Akbarnâme* of the wisdom and zealous faith of Father Aquaviva, the leader of this Jesuit mission, and relates how he offered to walk into a fiery furnace with a New Testament in his hand if the Mullahs would do the same with the Koran in their hand, but that the Mohammedan priests withdrew in terror before this test by fire. It is noteworthy in this connection that the Jesuits at Akbar's court received a warning from their superiors not to risk such rash experiments which might be induced by the devil with the view of bringing shame upon Christianity.[38] The superiors were apparently well informed with regard to the intentions of the devil.

In conversation with the Jesuits Akbar proved to be favorably inclined towards many of the Christian doctrines and met his guests half way in every manner possible. They had permission to erect a hospital and a chapel and to establish Christian worship in the latter for the benefit of the Portuguese in that vicinity. Akbar himself occasionally took part in this service kneeling with bared head, which, however, did not hinder him from joining also in the Mohammedan ritual or even the Brahman religious practices of the Rajput women in his harem. He had his second son Murâd instructed by the Jesuits in the Portuguese language and in the Christian faith.

The Jesuits on their side pushed energetically toward their goal and did not scorn to employ flattery in so far as to draw a parallel between the Emperor and Christ, but no matter how slyly the fathers proceeded in the accomplishment of their plans Akbar was always a match for them. In spite of all concessions with regard to the excellence and credibility of the Christian doctrines the Emperor never seemed to be entirely satisfied. Du Jarric "complains bitterly of his obstinacy and remarks that the restless intellect of this man could never be quieted by one answer but must constantly make further inquiry."[39] The clever historian of Islam makes the following comment: "Bad, very bad;—perhaps he would not even be satisfied with the seven riddles of the universe of the latest natural science."[40]

To every petition and importunity of the Jesuits to turn to Christianity Akbar maintained a firm opposition. A second and third embassy which the order at Goa sent out in the nineties of the sixteenth century, also labored in vain for Akbar's conversion in spite of the many evidences of favor shown by the Emperor. One of the last Jesuits to come, Jerome Xavier of Navarre, is said to have been induced by the Emperor to translate the four Gospels into Persian which was the language of the Mohammedan court of India. But Akbar never thought of allowing himself to be baptized, nor could he consider it seriously from political motives as well as from reasons of personal conviction. A man who ordered himself to be officially declared the highest authority in matters of faith—to be sure not so much in order to found an imperial papacy in his country as to guard his empire from an impending religious war—at any rate a man who saw how the prosperity of his reign proceeded from his own personal initiative in every respect, such a man could countenance no will above his own nor subject himself to any pangs of conscience. To recognize the Pope as highest authority and simply to recognize as objective truth a finally determined system in the realm in which he had spent day and night in a hot pursuit after a clearer vision, was for Akbar an absolute impossibility.

Then too Akbar could not but see through the Jesuits although he appreciated and admired many points about them. Their rigid dogmatism, their intolerance and inordinate ambition could leave him no doubt that if they once arose to power the activity of the Ulemâs, once by good fortune overthrown, would be again resumed by them to a stronger and more dangerous degree. It is also probable that Akbar, who saw and heard everything, had learned of the horrors of the Inquisition at Goa. Moreover, the clearness of Akbar's vision for the realities of national life had too often put him on his guard to permit him to look upon the introduction of Christianity, however highly esteemed by him personally, as a blessing for India. He had broken the power of Islam in India; to overthrow in like manner the second great religion of his empire, Brahmanism, to which the great majority of his subjects clung with body and soul, and then in place of both existing religions to introduce a third foreign religion inimically opposed to them—such a procedure would have hurled India into an irremediable confusion and destroyed at one blow the prosperity of the land which had been brought about by the ceaseless efforts of a lifetime. For of course it was not the aim of the Jesuits simply to win Akbar personally to Christianity but they wished to see their religion made the state religion of this great empire.

As has been already suggested, submission to Christianity would also have been opposed to Akbar's inmost conviction. He had climbed far enough up the stony path toward truth to recognize all religions as historically developed and as the products of their time and the land of their origin. All the nobler religions seemed to him to be radiations from the one eternal truth. That he thought he had found the truth with regard to the fate of the soul in the Sûfi-Vedântic doctrine of its migration through countless existences and its final ascension to deity has been previously mentioned. With such views Akbar could not become a Catholic Christian.

The conviction of the final reabsorption into deity, conditions also the belief in the emanation of the ego from deity. But Akbar's relation to God is not sufficiently identified with this belief. Akbar was convinced that he

stood nearer to God than other people. This is already apparent in the title "The Shadow of God" which he had assumed. The reversed, or rather the double, meaning of the sentence*Allâhu akbar*, "Akbar is God," was not displeasing to the Emperor as we know. And when the Hindus declared him to be an incarnation of a divinity he did not disclaim this homage. Such a conception was nothing unusual with the Hindus and did not signify a complete apotheosis. Although Akbar took great pains he was not able to permanently prevent the people from considering him a healer and a worker of miracles. But Akbar had too clear a head not to know that he was a man,—a man subject to mistakes and frailties; for when he permitted himself to be led into a deed of violence he had always experienced the bitterest remorse. Not the slightest symptom of Cæsaromania can be discovered in Akbar.

Akbar felt that he was a mediator between God and man and believed "that the deity revealed itself to him in the mystical illumination of his soul."

[41] This conviction Akbar held in common with many rulers of the Occident who were much smaller than he. Idolatrous marks of veneration he permitted only to a very limited

degree. He was not always quite consistent in this respect however, and we must realize how infinitely hard it was to be consistent in this matter at an Oriental court when the customary servility, combined with sincere admiration and reverence, longed to actively manifest itself.

Akbar, as we have already seen, suffered the Hindu custom of prostration, but on the other hand we have the express testimony to the contrary from the author Faizî, the trusted friend of the Emperor, who on the occasion of an exaggerated homage literally says: "The commands of His Majesty expressly forbid such devout reverence and as often as the courtiers offer homage of this kind because of their loyal sentiments His Majesty forbids them, for such manifestations of worship belong to God alone,"[42] Finally however Akbar felt himself moved to forbid prostration publicly, yet to permit it in a private manner, as appears in the following words of Abul Fazl[43]:

"But since obscurantists consider prostration to be a blasphemous adoration of man, His Majesty in his practical wisdom has commanded that it be put an end to with ignorant people of all stations and also that it shall not be practiced even by his trusted servants on public court days. Nevertheless if people upon whom the star of good fortune has shone are in attendance at private assemblies and receive permission to be seated, they may perform the prostration of gratitude by bowing their foreheads to the earth and so share in the rays of good fortune. So forbidding prostration to the people at large and granting it to the select the Emperor fulfils the wishes of both and gives the world an example of practical wisdom."

The desire to unite his subjects as much as possible finally impelled Akbar to the attempt to equalize religious differences as well. Convinced that religions did not differ from each other in their innermost essence, he combined what in his opinion were the essential elements and about the year 1580 founded a new religion, the famous Dîn i Ilâhi, the "religion of God." This religion recognizes only one God, a purely spiritual universally efficient being from whom the human soul is derived and towards which it tends. The ethics of this religion comprises the high moral requirements of Sufism and Parsism: complete toleration, equality of rights among all men, purity in thought, word and deed. The demand of monogamy, too, was added later. Priests, images and temples,—Akbar would have none of these in his new religion, but from the Parsees he took the worship of the fire and of the sun as to him light and its heat seemed the most beautiful symbol of the divine spirit.[44] He also adopted the holy cord of the Hindus and wore upon his forehead the colored token customary among them. In this eclectic manner he accommodated himself in a few externalities to the different religious communities existing in his kingdom.

Doubtless in the foundation of his Dîn i Ilâhi Akbar was not pursuing merely ideal ends but probably political ones as well, for the adoption of the new religion signified an increased loyalty to the Emperor. The novice had to declare himself ready to yield to the Emperor his property, his life, his honor, and his former faith, and in reality the adherents of the Dîn i Ilâhi formed a clan of the truest and most devoted servitors of the Emperor. It may not be without significance that soon after the establishment of the Dîn i Ilâhi a new computation of time was introduced which dated from the accession of Akbar to the throne in 1556.

After the new religion had been in existence perhaps five years the number of converts began to grow by the thousands but we can say with certainty that the greater portion of these changed sides not from conviction but on account of worldly advantage, since they saw that membership in the new religion was very advantageous to a career in the service of the state.[45] By far the greatest number of those who professed the Dîn i Ilâhi observed only the external forms, privately remaining alien to it.

MAUSOLEUM OF AKBAR AT SIKANDRA.

MAUSOLEUM OF AKBAR AT SIKANDRA.

In reality the new religion did not extend outside of Akbar's court and died out at his death. Hence if failure here can be charged to the account of the great Emperor, yet this very failure redounds to his honor. Must it not be counted as a great honor to Akbar that he considered it possible to win over his people to a spiritual imageless worship of God? Had he known that the religious requirements of the masses can only be satisfied by concrete objects of worship and by miracles (the more startling the better), that a spiritualized faith can never be the possession of any but a few chosen souls, he would not have proceeded with the founding of the Dîn i Ilâhi. And still we cannot call its establishment an absolute failure, for the spirit of tolerance which flowed out from Akbar's religion accomplished infinite good and certainly contributed just as much to lessening the antagonisms in India as did Akbar's social and industrial reforms.

A man who accomplished such great things and desired to accomplish greater, deserves a better fortune than was Akbar's towards the end of life. He had provided for his sons the most careful education, giving them at the same time Christian and orthodox Mohammedan instructors in order to lead them in their early years to the attainment of independent views by means of a comparison between contrasts; but he was never to have pleasure in his sons. It seems that he lacked the necessary severity. The two younger boys of this exceedingly temperate Emperor, Murâd and Daniâl, died of delirium tremens in their youth even before their father. The oldest son, Selim, later the Emperor Jehângir, was also a drunkard and was saved from destruction through this inherited vice of the Timur dynasty only by the wisdom and determination of his wife. But he remained a wild uncontrolled cruel man (as different as possible from his father and apparently so by intention) who took sides with the party of the vanquished Ulemâs and stepped forth as the restorer of Islam. In frequent open rebellion against his magnanimous father who was only too ready to pardon him, he brought upon this father the bitterest sorrow; and especially by having the trustworthy minister and friend of his father, Abul

Fazl, murdered while on a journey. Very close to Akbar also was the loss of his old mother to whom he had clung his whole life long with a touching love and whom he outlived only a short time.

Akbar lost his best friends and his most faithful servants before he finally succumbed to a very painful abdominal illness, which at the last changed him also mentally to a very sad extent, and finally carried him off on the night of the fifteenth of October, 1605. He was buried at Sikandra near Agra in a splendid mausoleum of enormous proportions which he himself had caused to be built and which even to-day stands almost uninjured.

This in short is a picture of the life and activities of the greatest ruler which the Orient has ever produced. In order to rightly appreciate Akbar's greatness we must bear in mind that in his empire he placed all men on an equality without regard to race or religion, and granted universal freedom of worship at a time when the Jews were still outlaws in the Occident and many bloody persecutions occurred from time to time; when in the Occident men were imprisoned, executed or burnt at the stake for the sake of their faith or their doubts; at a time when Europe was polluted by the horrors of witch-persecution and the massacre of St. Bartholemew.

[46] Under Akbar's rule India stood upon a much higher plane of civilization in the sixteenth century than Europe at the same time.

Germany should be proud that the personality of Akbar who according to his own words "desired to live at peace with all humanity, with every creature of God," has so inspired a noble German of princely blood in the last century that he consecrated the work of his life to the biography of Akbar. This man is the Prince Friedrich August of Schleswig-Holstein, Count of Noer, who wandered through the whole of Northern India on the track of Akbar's activities, and on the basis of the most careful investigation of sources has given us in his large two-volumed work the best and most extensive information which has been written in Europe about the Emperor Akbar. How much his work has been a labor of love can be recognized at every step in his book but especially may be seen in a touching letter from Agra written on the 24th of April, 1868, in which he relates that he utilized the early hours of this day for an excursion to lay a bunch of fresh roses on Akbar's grave and that no visit to any other grave had ever moved him so much as this.[47]

AKBAR - IMPEROR OF INDIA
HISTORIC FACTS

Reign	11 February 1556 – 27 October 1605[1][2]
Coronation	14 February 1556[1]
Predecessor	Humayun
Successor	Jahangir
Regent	Bairam Khan (1556–1561)
Wives	Ruqaiya Sultan Begum Salima Sultan Begum Mariam-uz-Zamani
Issue	Hassan Hussain Jahangir Murad Daniyal Aram Banu Begum Shakr-un-Nissa Begum Shahzadi Khanum others

Full name

Abu'l-Fath Jalal ud-din Muhammad Akbar

House	House of Timur
Father	Humayun
Mother	Hamida Banu Begum[3]
Born	Jalal ud-Din Muhammad 14 October 1542[4] Umerkot, Sindh
Died	27 October 1605 (aged 63) Fatehpur Sikri, Agra
Burial	Sikandra, Agra
Religion	Islam,[5] Din-e-Illahi

Abu'l-Fath Jalal ud-din Muhammad Akbar, known popularly as **Akbar** (IPA: [əkbər], literally "the great"; 14 October 1542 – 27 October 1605), also known as **Akbar the Great** or **Akbar I**,[6][7] was Mughal Emperor from 1556 until his death. He was the third and one of the greatest rulers of the Mughal Dynasty in India. Akbar succeeded his father, Humayun, under a regent, Bairam Khan, who helped the young emperor expand and consolidate Mughal domains in India. A strong personality and a successful general, Akbar gradually enlarged the Mughal Empire to include nearly all of the Indian Subcontinent north of the Godavari river. His power and influence, however, extended over the entire country because of Mughal military, political, cultural, and economic dominance. To unify the vast Mughal state, Akbar established a centralised system of administration throughout his empire and adopted a policy of conciliating conquered rulers through marriage and diplomacy. In order to preserve peace and order in a religiously and culturally diverse empire, he adopted policies that won him the support of his non-Muslim subjects. Eschewing tribal bonds and Islamic state identity, Akbar strived to unite far-flung lands of his realm through loyalty, expressed through a Persianised culture, to himself as an emperor who had near-divine status.

Mughal India developed a strong and stable economy, leading to commercial expansion and greater patronage of culture. Akbar himself was a patron of art and culture. He was fond of literature, and created a library of over 24,000 volumes written in Sanskrit, Hindustani, Persian, Greek, Latin, Arabic and Kashmiri, staffed by many scholars, translators, artists, calligraphers, scribes, bookbinders and readers. Holy men of many faiths, poets, architects and artisans adorned his court from all over the world for study and discussion. Akbar's courts at Delhi, Agra, and Fatehpur Sikri became centers of the arts, letters, and learning. Perso-Islamic culture began to merge and blend with indigenous Indian elements, and a distinct Indo-

Persian culture emerged characterised by Mughal style arts, painting, and architecture. Disillusioned with orthodox Islam and perhaps hoping to bring about religious unity within his empire, Akbar promulgated Din-i-Ilahi, a syncretic creed derived from Islam, Hinduism, Zoroastrianism, and Christianity. A simple, monotheistic cult, tolerant in outlook, it centered on Akbar as a prophet, for which he drew the ire of the ulema and orthodox Muslims.

Akbar's reign significantly influenced the course of Indian history. During his rule, the Mughal empire tripled in size and wealth. He created a powerful military system and instituted effective political and social reforms. By abolishing the sectarian tax on non-Muslims and appointing them to high civil and military posts, he was the first Mughal ruler to win the trust and loyalty of the native subjects. He had Sanskrit literature translated, participated in native festivals, realizing that a stable empire depended on the co-operation and good-will of his subjects. Thus, the foundations for a multicultural empire under Mughal rule was laid during his reign. Akbar was succeeded as emperor by his son, Jahangir

EARLY YEARS AND NAME

Akbar was born on 14 October 1542 (the fourth day of Rajab, 949 AH), at the Rajput Fortress of Umerkot in Sindh (in modern day Pakistan), where Prince Humayun and his recently wedded wife, Hamida Banu Begum, daughter of Shaikh Ali Akbar Jami, a Persian,[6] were given refuge by Rana Prasad, The then Rana of Umerkot.[8] After the capture of Kabul by Humayun, Badruddin's circumcision ceremony was held and his date of birth and name were changed to throw off evil sorcerers[9] and he was renamed Jalal-ud-din Muhammad by Humayun, a name which he had heard in his dream at Lahore.

Humayun had been driven into exile in Persia by the Pashtun leader Sher Shah Suri.[10] Akbar did not go to Persia with his parents, but was brought up in Kabul by the extended family of his paternal uncles, Kamran Mirza and Askari Mirza, and his aunts, in particular Kamran Mirza's wife. He spent his youth learning to hunt, run, and fight, made him a daring, powerful and a brave warrior, but he never learned to read or write. This, however, did not hinder his search for knowledge as it is said always when he retired in the evening he would have someone read.[11][better source needed] In November of 1551, Akbar married his first cousin, Ruqaiya Sultan Begum at Kabul.[12] Princess Ruqaiya was the only daughter of his paternal uncle, Hindal Mirza, and was his first wife and chief consort.[13] The marriage was arranged by Akbar's father and Ruqaiya's uncle, Emperor Humayun, and took place soon after the untimely death of Hindal Mirza, who died in a battle.[14]

Following the chaos over the succession of Sher Shah Suri's son Islam Shah, Humayun reconquered Delhi in 1555, leading an army partly provided by his Persian ally Tahmasp I. A few months later, Humayun died. Akbar's guardian, Bairam Khan concealed the death in order to prepare for Akbar's succession. Akbar succeeded Humayun on 14 February 1556, while in the midst of a war against Sikandar Shah to reclaim the Mughal throne. In Kalanaur, Punjab, the 13-year-old Akbar was enthroned by Bairam Khan on a newly constructed platform, which still stands.[15][16] He was proclaimed *Shahanshah* (Persian for "King of Kings"). Bairam Khan ruled on his behalf until he came of age.[17]

MILITARY CAMPAIGNS

MILITARY INNOVATIONS

Akbar was accorded the epithet "the Great" due to his many accomplishments,[18] among which was his record of unbeaten military campaigns that both established and consolidated Mughal rule in the Indian subcontinent. The basis of this military prowess and authority was Akbar's skillful structural and organisational calibration of the Mughal army.[19] The Mansabdari system in particular has been acclaimed for its role in upholding Mughal power in the time of Akbar. The system persisted with few changes down to the end of the Mughal Empire, but was progressively weakened under his successors.[19]

Organisational reforms were accompanied by innovations in cannons, fortifications, and the use of elephants.[18] Akbar also took an interest in matchlocks and effectively employed them during various conflicts. He sought the help of Ottomans, and also increasingly of Europeans, especially Portuguese and Italians, in procuring firearms and artillery.[20] Mughal firearms in the time of Akbar came to be far superior to anything that could be deployed by regional rulers, tributaries, or by zamindars.[21] Such was the impact of these weapons that Akbar's Vizier, Abul Fazl, once declared that "with the exception of Turkey, there is perhaps no country in which its guns has more means of securing the Government than [India]."[22] The term "Gunpower Empire" has thus often been used by scholars and historians in analysing the success of the Mughals in India. Mughal power has been seen as owing to their mastery of the techniques of warfare, especially the use of firearms encouraged by Akbar.[23]

STRUGGLE FOR NORTH INDIA

Akbar, who had been born in 1542 while his father, Humayun, was in flight from the victorious Surs, was only thirteen when he was proclaimed emperor in 1556. His father had succeeded in regaining control of the Punjab, Delhi, and Agra with Safavid support, but even in these areas Mughal rule was precarious, and when the Surs reconquered Agra and Delhi following the death of Humayun, the fate of the boy emperor seemed uncertain.

Akbar's minority and the lack of any possibility of militiary assistance from the Mughal stronghold of Kabul, that was at this time in the throes of an invasion by the ruler of Badakhshan, Prince Mirza Suleiman, aggravated the situation.[24] When his regent, Bairam Khan, called a council of war to marshall the Mughal forces, none of Akbar's chieftains approved of it. However, Bairam Khan was ultimately able to prevail over the nobles and it was decided that the Mughals would march against the strongest of the Sur rulers, Sikandar Shah Suri, in the Punjab. Delhi was left under the regency of Tardi Baig Khan.[24] Sikandar Shah Suri, however, presented no major concern for Akbar, and avoided giving battle as the Mughal army approached.[25] The gravest threat came from Hemu, a minister and general of one of the Sur rulers, who had proclaimed himself Hindu emperor and expelled the Mughals from the Indo-Gangetic plains.[24]

Urged by Bairam Khan, who re-marshalled the Mughal army before Hemu could consolidate his position, Akbar marched on Delhi to reclaim it.[26] Akbar's army, led by Bairam Khan, defeated Hemu and the Sur army on 5 November 1556 at the Second Battle of Panipat, 50 miles (80 km) north of Delhi.[27] Soon after the battle, Mughal forces occupied Delhi and then Agra. Akbar made a triumphant entry into Delhi, where he stayed for a month. Then he and Bairam Khan returned to Punjab, to deal with Sikandar Shah, who had become active again.[28] In the next six months, the Mughals won another major battle against Sikander Shah Suri, who then fled east to Bengal. Akbar and his forces occupied Lahore and then seized Multan in the Punjab. In 1558, Akbar took possession of Ajmer, the aperture to Rajputana, after the defeat and flight of its Muslim ruler.[28] Late in the same year, a Mughal commander defeated Ibrahim, the last Sur prince, and annexed Jaunpur, the capital of the former Sultanate of Jaunpur in the eastern Gangetic valley. The Mughals had also besieged and defeated the Sur forces in control of

Gwalior Fort, the greatest stronghold north of the Narmada river.[28]

The flurry of victories put the vital cities and strongholds located between Lahore, Delhi, Agra, and Jaunpur under Akbar's control.[28] This was Hindustan, the old heartland of Muslim Turko-Afghan political and military power in India. The Mughals, like their predecessors, were now poised to tap the immense agricultural productivity and trade potential of the epicenter of the Indo-Gangetic plains.[28] Royal begums, along with the families of Mughal amirs, were finally brought over from Kabul to India at the time—according to Akbar's vizier, Abul Fazl, "so that men might become settled and be restrained in some measure from departing to a country to which they were accustomed.[24] Akbar had firmly declared his intentions that the Mughals were in India to stay. This was a far cry from the political settlements by his grandfather, Babur, and by his father, Humayun, both of whom had done little to indicate that they were anything but transient rulers.[24][28]

EXPANSION INTO CENTRAL INDIA

By 1559, the Mughals had launched a drive to the south into Rajputana and Malwa.[29] However, Akbar's disputes with his regent, Bairam Khan, temporarily put an end to the expansion.[29] The young emperor, at the age of eighteen, wanted to take a more active part in managing affairs. Urged on by his foster mother, Maham Anga, and his relatives, Akbar decided to dispense with the services of Bairam Khan. After yet another dispute at court, Akbar finally dismissed Bairam Khan in the spring of 1560 and ordered him to leave on Hajj to Mecca.[30] Bairam Khan left for Mecca, but on his way was goaded by his opponents to rebel.[27] He was defeated by the Mughal army in the Punjab and forced to submit. Akbar, however forgave him and gave him the option of either continuing in his court or resuming his pilgrimage, of which Bairam chose the latter.[31] Bairam Khan was later assassinated on his way to

Mecca, allegedly by an Afghan with a personal vendetta.[29] In 1560, Akbar resumed military operations.[29] A Mughal army under the command of his foster brother, Adham Khan, and a Mughal commander, Pir Muhammad Khan, invaded Malwa. The Afghan ruler, Baz Bahadur, was defeated at the Battle of Sarangpur, and fled to Khandesh for refuge leaving behind his harem, treasure, and war elephants.[29] Despite initial success, the campaign proved a disaster from Akbar's point of view. His foster brother retained all the spoils and followed through with the Central Asian practice of slaughtering the surrendered garrison, their wives and children, and many Muslim theologians and Sayyids, who were the descendants of the Prophet Muhammad.[29] Akbar personally rode to Malwa to confront Adham Khan and relieve him of command. Pir Muhammad Khan was then sent in pursuit of Baz Bahadur but was beaten back by the alliance of the rulers of Khandesh and Berar.[29] Baz Bahadur temporarily regained control of Malwa until, in the next year, Akbar sent another Mughal army to invade and annex the kingdom.[29] Malwa became a province of the nascent imperial administration of Akbar's regime. Baz Bahadur survived as a refugee at various courts untils until, eight years later, in 1570, he took service under Akbar.[29]

Despite ultimate success in Malwa, the conflict however, exposed cracks in Akbar's personal relationships with his relatives and Mughal nobles. When Adham Khan confronted Akbar following another dispute in 1562, he was struck down by the emperor and thrown from a terrace into the palace courtyard at Agra. Still alive, Adham Khan was dragged up and thrown to the courtyard once again by Akbar to ensure his death. Akbar now sought to eliminate the threat of over-mighty subjects.[29] He created specialized ministerial posts relating to imperial governance. No member of the Mughal nobility was to have unquestioned pre-eminence.[29] When a powerful clan of Uzbek chiefs broke out in rebellion in 1564, Akbar decisively defeated and routed them in Malwa and then

Bihar.[32] He pardoned the rebellious leaders, hoping to conciliate them. But they rebelled again, so Akbar had to quell their uprising a second time. Following a third revolt with the proclamation of Mirza Muhammad Hakim, Akbar's brother and the Mughal ruler of Kabul, as emperor, his patience was finally exhausted. Several Uzbek chieftains were subsequently slain and the rebel leaders trampled to death under elephants.[32] Simultaneously the Mirza's, a group of Akbar's distant cousins who held important fiefs near Agra, had also risen up in rebellion. They, too were slain and driven out of the empire.[32] In 1566, Akbar moved to meet the forces of his brother, Muhammad Hakim, who had marched into the Punjab with dreams of seizing the imperial throne. Following a brief confontration, however, Muhammad Hakim accepted Akbar's supremacy and retreated back to Kabul.[32]

In 1564, Mughal forces conquered the Gondwana kingdom. Gondwana, a thinly populated hilly area in central India was of interest to the Mughals because of its herd of wild elephants.[33] The territory was ruled over by Raja Vir Narayan, a minor, and his mother, Durgavati, a Rajput warrior queen of the Gonds.[32] Akbar did not personally lead the campaign because he was preoccupied with the Uzbek rebellion, but left the expedition in the hands of Asaf Khan, the Mughal governor of Kara.[32][34] Durgavati committed suicide after her defeat at the Battle of Damoh while Raja Vir Narayan was slain at the Fall of Chauragarh, the mountain fortress of the Gonds.[34] The Mughals seized immense wealth, an uncalculated amount of gold and silver, jewels and 1000 elephants. Kamala Devi, a younger sister of Durgavati, was sent to the Mughal harem.[34] The brother of Durgavati's deceased husband was installed as the Mughal administrator of the region.[34] Like in Malwa, however, Akbar entered into a dispute with his vassals over the conquest of Gondwana.[34] Asaf Khan was accused of keeping most of the treasures, and sending back only 200 elephants to Akbar. When summoned to give accounts, he fled Gondwana. He went first to the Uzbeks, then returned to Gondwana where he was pursued by Mughal forces. Finally, he submitted and Akbar restored him to his previous position.[34]

CONQUEST OF RAJPUTANA

Having established Mughal rule over northern India, Akbar turned his attention to the conquest of Rajputana. No imperial power in India based on the Indo-Gangetic plains could be secure if a rival centre of power existed on its flank in Rajputana.[34] The Mughals had already established domination over parts of northern Rajputana in Mewar, Ajmer, and Nagor.[28][32] Now, however, Akbar was determined to drive into the heartlands of the Rajput kings that had never previously submitted to the Muslim rulers of the Delhi Sultanate. Beginning in 1561, the Mughals actively engaged the Rajputs in warfare and diplomacy.[33] Most Rajput states accepted Akbar's suzerainty; the ruler of Mewar, Udai Singh, however, remained outside the imperial fold.[32] Raja Udai Singh was descended from the Sisodia ruler, Rana Sanga, who had died fighting Babur at the Battle of Khanwa in 1527.[32] As the head of the Sisodia clan, he possessed the highest ritual status of all the Rajput kings and chieftains in India. Unless Udai Singh was reduced to submission, the imperial authority of the Mughals would be lessened in Rajput eyes.[32] Furthermore, Akbar, at this early period, was still enthusiastically devoted to the cause of Islam and sought to impress the superiority of his faith over the most prestigious warriors in Brahminical Hinduism.[32]

Bullocks dragging siege-guns up hill during Akbar's attack on Ranthambhor Fort in 1568

In 1567, Akbar moved to reduce the Chittorgarh Fort in Mewar. The fortress-capital of Mewar was of great strategic importance as it lay on the shortest route from Agra to Gujarat and was also considered a key to holding the interior parts of Rajputana. Udai Singh retired to the hills of Mewar, leaving two Rajput warriors, Jaimal and Patta, in charge of the defense of his capital.[35] Chittorgarh fell on February 1568 after a siege of four months. Akbar had the surviving defenders massacred and their heads displayed upon towers erected throughout the region, in order to demonstrate his authority.[36][37] The total loot that fell into the hands of the Mughals was distributed throughout the empire.[38] He remained in Chittorgarh for three days, then returned to Agra, where to commemorate the victory, he set up, at the gates of his fort, statues of Jaimal and Patta mounted on elephants.[39] Udai Singh's power and influence was broken. He never again ventured out his mountain refuge in Mewar and Akbar was content to let him be.[40]

The fall of Chittorgarh was followed up by a Mughal attack on the Ranthambore Fort in 1568. Ranthambore was held by the Hada Rajputs and reputed to be the most powerful fortress in India.[40] However, it fell only after a couple of months.[40] Akbar was now the master of almost the whole of Rajputana. Most of the Rajput kings had submitted to the Mughals.[40] Only the clans of Mewar continued to resist.[40] Udai Singh's son and successor, Pratap Singh, was later defeated by the Mughals at the Battle of Haldighati in 1576.[40] He spent the remainder of his life in exile in the Aravalli hills. Akbar would celebrate his conquest of Rajputana by laying the foundation of a new capital, 23 miles (37 km) W.S.W of Agra in 1569. It was called Fatehpur Sikri ("the city of victory").[41

ANNEXATION OF WESTERN AND EASTERN INDIA

Akbar's next military objectives were the conquest of Gujarat and Bengal, which connected India with the trading centres of Asia, Africa, and Europe through the Arabian Sea and the Bay of Bengal respectively.[40] Furthermore,

Gujarat had been a haven for rebellious Mughal nobles, while in Bengal, the Afghans still held considerable influence under their ruler, Sulaiman Khan Karrani. Akbar first moved against Gujarat, which lay in the crook of the Mughal provinces of Rajputana and Malwa.[40] Gujarat, with its coastal regions, possessed areas of rich agricultural production in its central plain; an impressive output of textiles and other industrial goods, and the busiest seaports of India.[40][42] Akbar intended to link the maritime state with the massive resources of the Indo-Gangetic plains.[43] However, the ostensible casus belli was that the rebel Mirzas, who had previously been driven out of India, were now operating out of a base in southern Gujarat. Morever, Akbar had received invitations from cliques in Gujarat to oust the reigning king, which served as justification for his military expedition.[40] In 1572, he moved to occupy Ahmedabad, the capital, and other northern cities, and was proclaimed the lawful sovereign of Gujarat. By 1573, he had driven out the Mirzas who, after offering token resistance, fled for refuge in the Deccan. Surat, the commercial capital of the region and other coastal cities soon capitulated to the Mughals.[40] The king, Muzaffar Shah III, was caught hiding in a corn field; he was pensioned off by Akbar with a small allowance.[40]

Having established his authority over Gujarat, Akbar returned to Fatephur Sikiri, where he built the Buland Darwaza to commemorate his victories, but a rebellion by Afghan nobles supported by the Rajput ruler of Idar, and the renewed intrigues of the Mirzas forced his return to Gujarat.[43] Akbar crossed the Rajputana and reached Ahmedabad in eleven days - a journey that normally took six weeks. The outnumbered Mughal army then won a decisive victory on 2 September 1573. Akbar slew the rebel leaders and erected a tower out of their severed heads.[40] The conquest and subjugation of Gujarat proved highly profitable for the Mughals; the territory yielded a revenue of more than five million rupees annually to Akbar's treasury, after expenses.[40]

Akbar had now defeated most of the Afghan remnants in India. The only centre of Afghan power was now in Bengal, where Sulaiman Khan Karrani, an Afghan chieftain whose family had served under Sher Shah Suri, was reigning in power. While Sulaiman Khan scrupulously avoided giving offence to Akbar, his son, Daud Khan, who had succeeded him in 1572, decided otherwise.[44] Whereas Sulaiman Khan had the khutba read in Akbar's name and acknowledged Mughal supremacy, Daud Khan assumed the insignia of royalty and ordered the khutba to be proclaimed in his own name in defiance of Akbar. Munim Khan, the Mughal governor of Bihar, was ordered to chastise Duad Khan, but later, Akbar himself set out to Bengal.[44] This was an opportunity to bring the trade in the east under Mughal control.[45] In 1574, the Mughals seized Patna from Daud Khan, who fled to Bengal.[44] Akbar returned to Fatehpur Sikri and left his generals to finish the campaign. The Mughal army was subsequently victorious at the Battle of Tukaroi in 1575, which led to the annexation of Bengal and parts of Bihar that had been under the dominion of Daud Khan. Only Orissa was left in the hands of the Karrani dynasty as a fief of the Mughal Empire. A year later, however, Daud Khan rebelled and attempted to regain Bengal. He was defeated by the Mughal general, Khan Jahan Quli, and had to flee into exile. Daud Khan was later captured and executed by Mughal forces. His severed head was sent to Akbar, while his limbs were gibbetted at Tandah, the Mughal capital in Bengal.[44]

CAMPAIGNS IN AFGHANISTAN AND CENTRAL ASIA

Following his conquests of Gujarat and Bengal, Akbar was preoccupied with domestic concerns. He did not leave Fatehpur Sikri on a military campaign until 1581, when the Punjab was again invaded by his brother, Mirza Muhammad Hakim.[44] Akbar expelled his brother to Kabul and this time pressed on, determined to end the threat from Muhammad Hakim once and for all.[44] In contrast to the problem that his predecessors once had in getting Mughal nobles to stay on in India, the problem now was to get them to leave India.[44] They were, according to Abul Fazl "afraid of the cold of Afghanistan."[44] The Hindu officers, in turn, were additionally inhibited by the traditional taboo against crossing the Indus. Akbar, however, spurred them on. The soldiers were provided with pay eight months in advance.[44] In August 1581, Akbar seized Kabul and took up residence at Babur's old citadel. He stayed there for three weeks, in the absence of his brother, who had fled into the mountains.[44] Akbar left Kabul in the hands of his sister, Bakht-un-Nisa Begum, and returned to India. He pardoned his brother, who took up de facto charge of the Mughal administration in Kabul; Bakht-un-Nis continued to be the official governor. A few years later, in 1585, Muhammad Hakim died and Kabul passed into the hands of Akbar once again. It was officially incorporated as a province of the Mughal Empire.[44]

The Kabul expedition was the beginning of a long period of activity over the northern frontiers of the empire.[46] For thirteen years, beginning in 1585, Akbar remained in the north, shifting his capital to Lahore in the Punjab while dealing with challenges from beyond the Khyber Pass.[46] The gravest threat came from the Uzbeks, the tribe that had driven his grandfather, Babur, out of Central Asia.[44] They had been organized under Abdullah Khan Shaybanid, a capable military chieftain who had seized Badakhshan and Balkh from Akbar's distant Timurid relatives, and whose Uzbek troops now posed a serious challenge to the northwestern frontiers of the Mughal Empire.[44][47] The Afghan tribes on the border were also restless, partly on account of the hostility of the Yusufzai of Bajaur and Swat, and partly owing to the activity of a new religious leader, Bayazid, the founder of the Roshaniyya sect.[46] The Uzbeks were also known to be subsidizing Afghans.[48]

In 1586, Akbar negotiated a pact with Abdullah Khan in which the Mughals agreed to remain neutral during the Uzbek invasion of Safavid held Khorasan.[48] In return, Abdullah Khan agreed to refrain from supporting, subsidizing, or offering refuge to the Afghan tribes hostile to the Mughals. Thus freed, Akbar began a series of campaigns to pacify the Yusufzais and other rebels.[48] Akbar ordered Zain Khan to lead an expedition against the Afghan tribes. Raja Birbal, a renowned minister in Akbar's court, was also given military command. The expedition turned out to be a disaster, and on its retreat from the mountains, Birbal and his entourage were ambushed and killed by the Afghans at the Malandarai Pass in February 1586.[48] Akbar immediately fielded new armies to reinvade the Yusufzai lands under the command of Raja Todar Mal. Over the next six years, the Mughals contained the Yusufzai in the mountain valleys, and forced the submission of many chiefs in Swat and Bajaur.[48] Dozens of forts were built and occupied to secure the region. Akbar's response demonstrated his ability to clamp firm military control over the Afghan tribes.[48]

Despite his pact with the Uzbeks, Akbar nurtured a secret hope of reconquering Central Asia from Afghanistan.[49] However, Badakshan and Balkh remained firmly part of the Uzbek dominions. There was only a transient occupation of the two provinces by the Mughals under his grandson, Shah Jahan, in the mid-17th century.[47] Nevertheless, Akbar's stay in the northern frontiers was highly fruitful. The last of the rebellious Afghan tribes were subdued by 1600.[47] The Roshaniyya movement was firmly suppressed. The Afridi and Orakzai tribes, which had risen up under the Roshaniyyas, had been subjugated.[47] The leaders of the movement were captured and driven into exile.[47] Jalaluddin, the son of the Roshaniyya movement's founder, Bayazid, was killed in 1601 in a fight with Mughal troops near Ghazni.[47] Mughal rule over Afghanistan was finally secure, particularly after the passing of the Uzbek threat with the death of Abdullah Khan in 1598.[48]

CONQUESTS IN THE INDUS VALLEY

While in Lahore dealing with the Uzbeks, Akbar had sought to subjugate the Indus valley to secure the frontier provinces.[48] He sent an army to conquer Kashmir in the upper Indus basin when, in 1585, Ali Shah, the reigning king of the Shia Chak dynasty, refused to send his son as a hostage to the Mughal court. Ali Shah surrendered immediately to the Mughals, but another of his sons, Yaqub, crowned himself as king, and led a stubborn resistance to Mughal armies. Finally, in June, 1589, Akbar himself travelled from Lahore to Srinagar to receive the surrender of Yaqub and his rebel forces.[48] Baltistan and Ladakh, which were Tibetan provinces adjacent to Kashmir, pledged their allegiance to Akbar.[50] The Mughals also moved to conquer Sindh in the lower Indus valley. Since 1574, the northern fortress of Bhakkar had remained under imperial control. Now, in 1586, the Mughal governor of Multan tried and failed to secure the capitulation of Mirza Jani Beg, the independent ruler of Thatta in southern Sindh.[48] Akbar responded by sending a Mughal army to besiege Sehwan, the river capital of the region. Jani Beg mustered a large army to meet the Mughals.[48] The outnumbered Mughal forces defeated the Sindhi forces at the Battle of Sehwan. After suffering further defeats, Jani Beg surrendered to the Mughals in 1591, and in 1593, paid homage to Akbar in Lahore.[50]

SUBJUGATION OF BALUCHISTAN

As early as 1586, about half a dozen Baluchi chiefs had been persuaded to attend the imperial court and acknowledge the vassalage of Akbar. In preparations to take Kandahar from the Safavids, Akbar ordered the Mughal forces to conquer the rest of Baluchistan in 1595.[50][51] The Mughal general, Mir Masum, led an attack on the stronghold of Sibi, situated to the northwest of Quetta and defeated a coalition of local chieftains in a pitched battle.[51] They were made to acknowledge Mughal supremacy and attend Akbar's court. As a result, the whole of Baluchistan, including the strategic region of Makran, the coastal strip running from India to Iran, became a part of the Mughal Empire.[51] The Mughals now frontiered Persian ruled Kandahar from three sides.[51]

SAFAVIDS AND KANDAHAR

Kandahar was the name given by Arab historians to the ancient Indian kingdom of Gandhara.[52] It was intimately connected with the Mughals since the time of their ancestor, Timur, the warlord who had conquered much of South, Central, and Western Asia in the 14th century. However, the Safavids considered it as an appanage of the Persian ruled territory of Khorasan and declared its association with the Mughal emperors to be a usurpation. In 1558, while Akbar was consolidating his rule over northern India, the Safavid emperor, Tahmasp I, had seized Kandahar and expelled its Mughal governor. For the next thirty years, it remained under Persian rule.[50] The recovery of Kandahar had not been a priority for Akbar, but after his prolonged military activity in the northern frontiers, a move to restore Mughal rule over the region became desirable.[50] The conquests of Sindh, Kashmir and Baluchisan, and the ongoing consolidation of Mughal power over Afghanistan had added to Akbar's confidence.[50] Furthermore, Kandahar was at this time under threat from the Uzbeks, but the Emperor of Persia, himself beleaguered by the Ottoman Turks, was unable to send any reinforcements. Circumstances favoured the Mughals.[50]

In 1593, Akbar received the exiled Safavid prince, Rostam Mirza, after he had quarelled with his family.[53] Rostam Mirza pledged allegiance to the Mughals; he was granted a rank (mansab) of commander of 5000 men and received Multan as a jagir.[53] Beleaguered by constant Uzbek raids, and seeing the reception of Rostom Mirza at the Mughal court, the Safavid prince and governor of Kandahar,

Mozaffar Hosayn, also agreed to defect to the Mughals. Mozaffar Hosayn, who was in any case in an adversary relationship with his overlord, Shah Abbas, was granted a rank of 5000 men, and his daughter was married to Akbar's grandson, the Mughal prince, Khurram.[50][53] Kandahar was finally secured in 1595 with the arrival of a garrison headed by the Mughal general, Shah Bayg Khan.[53] The reconquest of Kandahar did not overtly disturb the Mughal-Persian relationship.[50] Akbar and the Persian Shah continued to exchange ambassadors and presents. However, the power equation between the two had now changed in favour of the Mughals.[50] Akbar had built a large and secure empire for himself, while Persian power had declined.[50]

ADMINISTRATION

POLITICAL GOVERNMENT

Akbar's system of central government was based on the system that had evolved since the Delhi Sultanate, but the functions of various departments were carefully reorganised by laying down detailed regulations for their functioning

> The revenue department was headed by a *wazir*, responsible for all finances and management of *jagir* and *inam* lands.
> The head of the military was called the *mir bakshi*, appointed from among the leading nobles of the court. The *mir bakshi* was in charge of intelligence gathering, and also made recommendations to the emperor for military appointments and promotions.
> The *mir saman* was in charge of the imperial household, including the harems, and supervised the functioning of the court and royal bodyguard.
> The judiciary was a separate organization headed by a chief *qazi*, who was also responsible for religious beliefs and practices

TAXATION

Akbar set about reforming the administration of his empire's land revenue by adopting a system that had been used by Sher Shah Suri. A cultivated area where crops grew well was measured and taxed through fixed rates based on the area's crop and productivity. However, this placed hardship on the peasantry because tax rates were fixed on the basis of prices prevailing in the imperial court, which were often higher than those in the countryside.[54] Akbar changed to a decentralized system of annual assessment, but this resulted in corruption among local officials and was abandoned in 1580, to be replaced by a system called the *dahsala*.[55] Under the new system, revenue was calculated as one-third of the average produce of the previous ten years, to be paid to the state in cash. This system was later refined, taking into account local prices, and grouping areas with similar productivity into assessment circles. Remission was given to peasants when the harvest failed during times of flood or drought.[55] Akbar's *dahsala* system is credited to Raja Todar Mal, who also served as a revenue officer under Sher Shah Suri,[56] and the structure of the revenue administration was set out by the latter in a detailed memorandum submitted to the emperor in 1582-83.[57]

Other local methods of assessment continued in some areas. Land which was fallow or uncultivated was charged at concessional rates.[58] Akbar also actively encouraged the improvement and extension of agriculture. The village continued to remain the primary unit of revenue assessment.[59] Zamindars of every area were required to provide loans and agricultural implements in times of need, to encourage farmers to plough as much land as possible and to sow seeds of superior quality. In turn, the zamindars were given a hereditary right to collect a share of the produce. Peasants had a hereditary right to cultivate the land as long as they paid the land revenue.[58] While the revenue assessment system showed concern for the small peasantry, it also maintained a level of distrust towards the revenue officials. Revenue officials were guaranteed only three-quarters of their salary, with the remaining quarter dependent on their full realisation of the revenue assessed.[60]

MILITARY ORGANIZATION

Main article: Mansabdari

> *An Emperor shall be ever Intent on Conquest, Otherwise His enemies shall rise in arms against him.*
>
> **Jalal-ud-Din Muhammad Akbar**,

Akbar organized his army as well as the nobility by means of a system called the *mansabdari*. Under this system, each officer in the army was assigned a rank (a *mansabdar*), and assigned a number of cavalry that he had to supply to the imperial army.[56] The *mansabdars* were divided into 33 classes. The top three commanding ranks, ranging from 7000 to 10000 troops, were normally reserved for princes. Other ranks between 10 and 5000 were assigned to other members of the nobility. The empire's permanent standing army was quite small and the imperial forces mostly consisted of contingents maintained by the *mansabdars*.[61] Persons were normally appointed to a low *mansab* and then promoted, based on their merit as well as the favour of the emperor.[62] Each *mansabdar* was required to maintain a certain number of cavalrymen and twice that number of horses. The number of horses was greater because they had to be rested and rapidly replaced in times of war. Akbar employed strict measures to ensure that the quality of the armed forces was maintained at a high level; horses were regularly inspected and only Arabian horses were normally employed.[63] The *mansabdars* were remunerated well for their services and constituted the highest paid military service in the world at the time.[62]

CAPITAL

Akbar was a follower of Salim Chishti, a holy man who lived in the region of Sikri near Agra. Believing the area to be a lucky one for himself, he had a mosque constructed there for the use of the priest. Subsequently, he celebrated the victories over Chittor and Ranthambore by laying the foundation of a new walled capital, 23 miles (37 km) west of Agra in 1569, which was named Fatehpur ("*town of victory*") after the conquest of Gujarat in 1573 and subsequently came to be known as Fatehpur Sikri in order to distinguish it from other similarly named towns.[35] Palaces for each of Akbar's senior queens, a huge artificial lake, and sumptuous water-filled courtyards were built there. However, the city was soon abandoned and the capital was moved to Lahore in 1585. The reason may have been that the water supply in Fatehpur Sikri was insufficient or of poor quality. Or, as some historians believe, Akbar had to attend to the northwest areas of his empire and therefore moved his capital northwest. Other sources indicate Akbar simply lost interest in the city[64] or realised it was not militarily defensible. In 1599, Akbar shifted his capital back to Agra from where he reigned until his death.

ECONOMY

TRADE

The reign of Akbar was characterised by commercial expansion.[65] The Mughal government encouraged traders, provided protection and security for transactions, and levied a very low custom duty to stimulate foreign trade. Furthermore, it strived to foster a climate conductive to commerce by requing local administrators to provide restitution to traders for goods stolen while in their territory.

In order to minimize such incidents, bands of highway police called *rahdars* were enlisted to parol roads and ensure safety of traders. Other active measures taken included the construction and protection of routes of commerce and communications.[66] Indeed, Akbar would make concerted efforts to improve roads to facilitate the use of wheeled vehicles through the Khyber Pass, the most popular route frequented by traders and travellers in journeying from Kabul into Mughal India.[66] He also strategically occupied the northwestern cities of Multan and Lahore in the Punjab and constructed great forts, such as the one at Attock near the crossing of the Grand Trunk Road and the Indus river, as well as a network of smaller forts called *thanas* throughout the frontier to secure the overland trade with Persia and Central Asia.[66]

COINS

Akbar was a great innovator as far as coinage in concerned. The coins of Akbar set a new chapter in India's numismatic history. The coins of Akbar's grandfather, Babur, and father, Humayun, are basic and devoid of any innovation as the former was busy establishing the foundations of the Mughal rule in India while the latter was ousted by the Afghan, Farid Khan Sher Shah Suri, and returned to the throne only to die a year later. While the reign of both Babur and Humayun represented turmoil, Akbar's relative long reign of 50 years allowed him to experiment with coinage.

Akbar introduced coins with decorative floral motifs, dotted borders, quatrefoil and other types. His coins were both round and square in shape with a unique 'mehrab' (lozenge) shape coin highlighting numismatic calligraphy at its best. Akbar's portrait type gold coin (Mohur) is generally attributed to his son, Prince Salim (later Emperor Jahangir), who had rebelled and then sought reconciliation thereafter by minting and presenting his father with gold Mohur's bearing Akbar's portrait. The tolerant view of

Akbar is represented by the 'Ram-Siya' silver coin type while during the latter part of Akbar's reign, we see coins portraying the concept of Akbar's newly promoted religion 'Din-e-ilahi' with the Ilahi type and Jalla Jalal-Hu type coins.

Silver coin of Akbar with inscriptions of the Islamic declaration of faith, the declaration reads: "There is no god but God, and Muhammad is the messenger of Allah."

The coins, left, represent examples of these innovative concepts introduced by Akbar that set the precedent for Mughal coins which was refined and perfected by his son, Jahangir, and later by his grandson, Shah Jahan.

DIPLOMACY

MATRIMONIAL ALLIANCES

The practice of giving Hindu princesses to Muslim kings in marriage was known much before Akbar's time, but in most cases these marriages did not lead to any stable relations between the families involved, and the women were lost to their families and did not return after marriage.[67][68]

However, Akbar's policy of matrimonial alliances marked a departure in India from previous practice in that the marriage itself marked the beginning of a new order of relations, wherein the Hindu Rajputs who married their daughters or sisters to him would be treated on par with his Muslim fathers-in-law and brothers in-law in all respects except being able to dine and pray with him or take Muslim wives. These Rajputs were made members of his court and their daughters' or sisters' marriage to a Muslim ceased to be a sign of degradation, except for certain proud elements who still considered it a sign of humiliation.[68]

The Kacchwaha Rajput, Raja Bharmal, of Amber, who had come to Akbar's court shortly after the latter's accession, entered into an alliance by giving his daughter Harkha Bai in marriage to the emperor. There has been considerable discussion among historians whether Harka bai or Rajkumari Hira Kunwari, the wife of Akbar and the daughter of Raja Bharmal of Amber, is the Jodha bai or not. Tuzk-e-Jahangiri, the autobiography of Jahangir, doesn't mention Jodha Bai.[69] Therein, she is referred to as Mariam uz Zamani.[70] Neither the Akbarnama (a biography of Akbar commissioned by Akbar himself), nor any historical text from the period refer to her as Jodha Bai.[70][71][72] She died in 1623. A mosque was built in her honor by her son Jahangir in Lahore.[73] Bharmal was made a noble of high rank in the imperial court, and subsequently his son Bhagwant Das and grandson Man Singh also rose to high ranks in the nobility.[67]

Other Rajput kingdoms also established matrimonial alliances with Akbar, but matrimony was not insisted on as a precondition for forming alliances. Two major Rajput clans remained aloof – the Sisodiyas of Mewar and Hadas of Ranthambore. In another turning point of Akbar's reign, Raja Man Singh I of Amber went with Akbar to meet the Hada leader, Surjan Hada, to effect an alliance. Surjan accepted an alliance on the condition that Akbar did not marry any of his daughters. Consequently, no matrimonial alliance was entered into, yet Surjan was made a noble and placed in charge of Garh-Katanga.[67] Certain other Rajput nobles did not like the idea of their kings marrying their daughters to Mughals. Rathore Kalyandas threatened to kill both Mota Raja Rao Udaisingh and Jahangir because Udai Singh had decided to marry his daughter to Jahangir. Akbar on hearing this ordered imperial forces to attack Kalyandas at Siwana. Kalyandas died fighting along with his men and the women of Siwana committed Jauhar.[74]

The political effect of these alliances was significant. While some Rajput women who entered Akbar's harem converted to Islam, they were generally provided full religious freedom, and their relatives, who continued to remain Hindu, formed a significant part of the nobility and served to articulate the opinions of the majority of the common populace in the imperial court.[67] The interaction between Hindu and Muslim nobles in the imperial court resulted in exchange of thoughts and blending of the two cultures. Further, newer generations of the Mughal line represented a merger of Mughal and Rajput blood, thereby strengthening ties between the two. As a result, the Rajputs became the strongest allies of the Mughals, and Rajput soldiers and generals fought for the Mughal army under Akbar, leading it in several campaigns including the conquest of Gujarat in 1572.[75] Akbar's policy of religious tolerance ensured that employment in the imperial administration was open to all on merit irrespective of creed, and this led to an increase in the strength of the administrative services of the empire.[76]

Another legend is that Akbar's daughter Meherunnissa was enamoured by Tansen and had a role in his coming to Akbar's court.[77] Tansen converted to Islam from Hinduism, apparently on the eve of his marriage with Akbar's daughter.[78][79]

FOREIGN RELATIONS

Relations with the Portuguese

At the time of Akbar's ascension in 1556, the Portuguese had established several fortresses and factories on the western coast of the subcontinent, and largely controlled navigation and sea-trade in that region. As a consequence of this colonialism, all other trading entities were subject to the terms and conditions of the Portuguese, and this was resented by the rulers and traders of the time including Bahadur Shah of Gujarat.[81]

In the year 1572 the Mughal Empire annexed Gujarat and acquired its first access to the sea, the local officials informed Akbar that the Portuguese have begun to exert their control in the Indian Ocean. Hence Akbar was conscious of the threat posed by the presence of the Portuguese, remained content with obtaining a *cartaz* (permit) from them for sailing in the Persian Gulf region.[82] At the initial meeting of the Mughals and the Portuguese during the Siege of Surat in 1572, the Portuguese, recognising the superior strength of the Mughal army, chose to adopt diplomacy instead of war, and the Portuguese Governor, upon the request of Akbar, sent him an ambassador to establish friendly relations.[83] Akbar's efforts to purchase and secure from the Portuguese some of their compact Artillery pieces were unsuccessful and that is the reason why Akbar could not establish the Mughal navy along the Gujarat coast.[84]

Akbar accepted the offer of diplomacy, but the Portuguese continually acknowledged their authority and power in the Indian Ocean, in fact Akbar was highly concerned when he had to request a permit from the Portuguese before any ships from the Mughal Empire were to depart for the Hajj pilgrimage to Mecca and Medina.[85] In 1573, he issued a *firman* directing Mughal administrative officials in Gujarat not to provoke the Portuguese in the territory they held in Daman. The Portuguese, in turn, issued passes for the members of Akbar's family to go on Hajj to Mecca. The Portuguese made mention of the extraordinary status of the vessel and the special status to be accorded to its occupants.[86]

In the year 1579 Jesuits from Goa were allowed to visit the court of Akbar, and he had his scribes translate the New Testament, and granted the Jesuits freedom to make converts and raise one of his sons.[87] The Jesuit did not confine themselves to the exposition of their own beliefs, but reviled Islam and the Prophet in unrestrained language. Their comments enraging the Imam's and Ulama, who objected to the remarks of the Jesuit, but Akbar however ordered their comments to be recorded and observed the Jesuits and their behavior carefully. This event was followed by a rebellion of Muslim clerics led by Mullah Muhammad Yazdi and Muiz-ul-Mulk, the chief Qadi of Bengal in the year 1581, when these rebels wanted to overthrow Akbar and insert his brother Mirza Muhammad Hakim ruler of Kabul on the Mughal throne. Akbar however successfully defeated the rebels and had grown more cautious about his guests and his proclamations, which he later checked with his advisers carefully.[88]

RELATIONS WITH THE OTTOMAN EMPIRE

In the year 1555, while Akbar was still a child the Ottoman Admiral Seydi Ali Reis visited the Mughal Emperor Humayun. Later in the year 1569, during the early years of Akbar's rule another Ottoman Admiral Kurtoğlu Hızır Reis arrived on the shores of the Mughal Empire. These Ottoman Admirals sought to end the growing threats of the Portuguese Empire during their Indian Ocean campaigns. During his reign Akbar himself is known to have sent six documents addressing the Ottoman Sultan Suleiman the Magnificent.[89][90]

In 1576 Akbar sent a very large contingent of pilgrims led by Khwaja Sultan Naqshbandi, Yahya Saleh, with 600,000 gold and silver coins and 12,000 Kaftans of honor and large consignments of rice.[91] In October 1576, the Mughal Emperor Akbar, sent a delegation including members of his family including his aunt Gulbadan Begum and his consort Salima, on Hajj by two ships from Surat including an Ottoman vessel, which reached the port of Jeddah in 1577 and then proceeded towards Mecca and Medina.[92] Four more caravans were sent from 1577 to 1580, with exquisite gifts for the authorities of Mecca and Medina.[93][94]

The imperial Mughal entourage stayed in Mecca and Medina for nearly four years, and attended the Hajj four times. During this period Akbar even financed the pilgrimages of many poor Muslims from the Mughal Empire and also funded the foundations of the Qadiriyya Sufi Order's dervish lodge in the Hijaz.[95] The Mughals eventually set out for Surat and their return was assisted by the Ottoman Pasha in Jeddah.[96] Due to Akbar's attempts to build Mughal presence in Mecca and Medina, the local Sharif's began to have more confidence in the financial support provided by Mughal Empire, this lessened their dependency upon Ottoman bounty.[95] Mughal-Ottoman trade also flourished during this period, in fact merchants loyal to Akbar are known to have reached and sold spices, dyestuff, cotton and shawls in the Bazaars of Aleppo after arriving and journeying upriver through the port of Basra.[97]

According to some accounts Mughal Emperor Akbar expressed a desire to form an alliance with the Portuguese, mainly in order to advance his interests, but whenever the Portuguese attempted to invade the Ottomans, the Mughal Emperor Akbar proved abortive.[98][99] In 1587 a Portuguese fleet sent to attack Yemen was ferociously routed and defeated by the Ottoman Navy; thereafter the Mughal-Portuguese alliance immediately collapsed mainly because of the continuing pressure by the Mughal Empire's prestigious vassals at Janjira.[100]

RELATIONS WITH THE SAFAVID DYNASTY

The Safavids and the Mughals had a long history of diplomatic relationship, with the Safavid ruler Tahmasp I having provided refuge to Humayun when he had to flee the Indian subcontinent following his defeat by Sher Shah Suri. During the 16th and 17th centuries, the two empires, along with the Ottoman Empire to the west, were the site of major power struggles in Asia. However, the Safavids differed from the Mughals and the Ottomans in following the Shiite sect of Islam as opposed to the Sunni sect practised by the other two.[101] One of the longest standing disputes between the Safavids and the Mughals pertained to the control of the city of Qandahar in the Hindukush region, forming the border between the two empires.[102] The Hindukush region was militarily very significant owing to its geography, and this was well-recognised by strategists of the times.[103] Consequently, the city, which was being administered by Bairam Khan at the time of Akbar's accession, was invaded and captured by the Persian ruler Husain Mirza, a cousin of Tahmasp I, in 1558.[102] Subsequent to this, Bairam Khan sent an envoy to Tahmasp I's court, in an effort to maintain peaceful relations with the Safavids. This gesture was reciprocated and a cordial relationship continued to prevail between the two empires during the first two decades of Akbar's reign.[104] However, the death of Tahmasp I in 1576 resulted in civil war and instability in the Safavid empire, and diplomatic relations between the two empires ceased for more than a decade, and were restored only in 1587 following the accession of Shah Abbas to the Safavid throne.[105] Shortly afterwards, Akbar's army completed its annexation of Kabul, and in order to further secure the north-western boundaries of his empire, it proceeded to Qandahar. The city capitulated without resistance on 18 April 1595, and the ruler Muzaffar Hussain moved into Akbar's court.[106] Qandahar continued to remain in Mughal possession, and the Hindukush the empire's western frontier, for several decades until Shah Jahan's expedition into Badakhshan in 1646.[107] Diplomatic relations continued to be maintained between the Safavid and Mughal courts until the end of Akbar's reign.[108]

RELATIONS WITH OTHER CONTEMPORARY KINGDOMS

Vincent Arthur Smith observes that the merchant Mildenhall was employed in 1600 while the establishment of the Company was under adjustment to bear a letter from Queen Elizabeth to Akbar requesting liberty to trade in his dominions on terms as good as those enjoyed by the Portuguese.[109]

Akbar was also visited by the French explorer Pierre Malherbe.[110]

RELIGIOUS POLICY

Akbar, as well as his mother and other members of his family, are believed to have been Sunni Hanafi Muslims.[111] His early days were spent in the backdrop of an atmosphere in which liberal sentiments were encouraged and religious narrow-mindedness was frowned upon.[112] From the 15th century, a number of rulers in various parts of the country adopted a more liberal policy of religious tolerance, attempting to foster communal harmony between Hindus and Muslims.[113] These sentiments were earlier encouraged by the teachings of popular saints like Guru Nanak, Kabir and Chaitanya,[112] the verses of the Persian poet Hafez which advocated human sympathy and a liberal outlook,[114] as well as the Timurid ethos of religious tolerance in the empire, persisted in the polity right from the times of Timur to Humayun, (the second emperor of the mughal empire), and influenced Akbar's policy of tolerance in matters of religion.[115] Further, his childhood tutors, who included two Irani Shias, were largely above sectarian prejudices, and made a significant contribution to Akbar's later inclination towards religious tolerance.[115]

When he was at Fatehpur Sikri, he held discussions as he loved to know about others' religious beliefs. On one such day he got to know that the religious people of other religions were often bigots (intolerant of others religious beliefs). This led him to form the idea of the new religion, Sulh-e-kul meaning universal peace. His idea of this religion did not discriminate other religions and focused on the ideas of peace, unity and tolerance.[citation needed]

ASSOCIATION WITH THE MUSLIM ARISTOCRACY

During the early part of his reign, Akbar adopted an attitude of suppression towards Muslim sects that were condemned by the orthodoxy as heretical.[116] In 1567, on the advice of Shaikh Abdu'n Nabi, he ordered the exhumation of Mir Murtaza Sharifi Shirazi - a Shia buried in Delhi - because of the grave's proximity to that of Amir Khusrau, arguing that a "heretic" could not be buried so close to the grave of a Sunni saint, reflecting a restrictive attitude towards the Shia, which continued to persist till the early 1570s.[117] He suppressed Mahdavism in 1573 during his campaign in Gujarat, in the course of which the Mahdavi leader Bandagi Miyan Sheik Mustafa was arrested and brought in chains to the court for debate and released after eighteen months.[117] However, as Akbar increasingly came under the influence of pantheistic Sufi mysticism from the early 1570s, it caused a great shift in his outlook and culminated in his shift from orthodox Islam as traditionally professed, in favor of a new concept of Islam transcending the limits of religion.[117] Consequently, during the latter half of his reign, he adopted a policy of tolerance towards the Shias and declared a prohibition on Shia-Sunni conflict, and the empire remained neutral in matters of internal sectarian conflict.[118] In the year 1578, the Mughal Emperor Akbar famously referred to himself as:

" *Emperor of Islam, Emir of the Faithful, Shadow of God on earth, Abul Fath Jalal-ud-din Muhammad Akbar Badshah Ghazi (whose empire Allah perpetuate), is a* " *most just, most wise, and a most God-fearing ruler.*

In 1580, a rebellion broke out in the eastern part of Akbar's empire, and a number of *fatwas*, declaring Akbar to be a heretic, were issued by Qazis. Akbar suppressed the rebellion and handed out severe punishments to the Qazis. In order to further strengthen his position in dealing with the Qazis, Akbar issued a *mazhar* or declaration that was signed by all major *ulemas* in 1579.[119][120] The *mahzar* asserted that Akbar was the *Khalifa* of the age, the rank of the *Khalifa* was higher than that of a *Mujtahid*, in case of a difference of opinion among the Mujtahids, Akbar could select any one opinion and could also issue decrees which did not go against the *nass*.[121] Given the prevailing Islamic sectarian conflicts in various parts of the country at that time, it is believed that the *Mazhar* helped in stabilizing the religious situation in the empire.[119] It made Akbar very powerful due to the complete supremacy accorded to the *Khalifa* by Islam, and also helped him eliminate the religious and political influence of the Ottoman *Khalifa* over his subjects, thus ensuring their complete loyalty to him.[122]

Throughout his reign the Mughal Emperor Akbar was a patron of influential Muslim scholars such as Mir Ahmed Nasrallah Thattvi and Tahir Muhammad Thattvi.[citation needed]

Whenever the Mughal Emperor Akbar would attend congregations at a Mosque the following proclamation was made:[123]

" *The Lord to me the Kingdom gave, He made me wise, strong and brave, He guides me through right and truth, Filling my mind with the love of truth, No praise of man could sum his state, Allah Hu Akbar, God is Great.* "

DIN-I-ILAHI

Akbar was deeply interested in religious and philosophical matters. An orthodox Muslim at the outset, he later came to be influenced by Sufi mysticism that was being preached in the country at that time, and moved away from orthodoxy, appointing to his court several talented people with liberal ideas, including Abul Fazl, Faizi and Birbal. In 1575, he built a hall called the Ibadat Khana (*"House of Worship"*) at Fatehpur Sikri, to which he invited theologians, mystics and selected courtiers renowned for their intellectual achievements and discussed matters of spirituality with them.[112] These discussions, initially restricted to Muslims, were acrimonious and resulted in the participants shouting at and abusing each other. Upset by this, Akbar opened the Ibadat Khana to people of all religions as well as atheists, resulting in the scope of the discussions broadening and extending even into areas such as the validity of the Quran and the nature of God. This shocked the orthodox theologians, who sought to discredit Akbar by circulating rumours of his desire to forsake Islam.[119]

Akbar's effort to evolve a meeting point among the representatives of various religions was not very successful, as each of them attempted to assert the superiority of their respective religions by denouncing other religions. Meanwhile, the debates at the Ibadat Khana grew more acrimonious and, contrary to their purpose of leading to a better understanding among religions, instead led to greater bitterness among them, resulting to the discontinuance of the debates by Akbar in 1582.[124] However, his interaction with various religious theologians had convinced him that despite their differences, all religions had several good practices, which he sought to combine into a new religious movement known as Din-i-Ilahi.[125][126] However, some modern scholars claim that Akbar did not initiate a new religion and did not use the word *Din-i-Ilahi*.[127] According to the contemporary events in the Mughal court Akbar was indeed angered by the acts of embezzlement of wealth by many high level Muslim clerics.[128]

The purported Din-i-Ilahi was more of an ethical system and is said to have prohibited lust, sensuality, slander and pride, considering them sins. Piety, prudence, abstinence and kindness are the core virtues. The soul is encouraged to purify itself through yearning of God.[129] Celibacy was respected, chastity enforced, the slaughter of animals was forbidden and there were no sacred scriptures or a priestly hierarchy.[130] However, a leading Noble of Akbar's court, Aziz Koka, wrote a letter to him from Mecca in 1594 arguing that the discipleship promoted by Akbar amounted to nothing more than a desire on Akbar's part to portray his superiority regarding religious matters.[131] To commemorate Din-e-Ilahi, he changed the name of Prayag to Allahabad (pronounced as *ilahabad*) in 1583.[132][133]

It has been argued that the theory of Din-i-Ilahi being a new religion was a misconception which arose due to erroneous translations of Abul Fazl's work by later British historians.[134] However, it is also accepted that the policy of *sulh-e-kul*, which formed the essence of Din-i-Ilahi, was adopted by Akbar not merely for religious purposes, but as a part of general imperial administrative policy. This also formed the basis for Akbar's policy of religious toleration.[135] At the time of Akbar's death in 1605 there were no signs of discontent amongst his Muslim subjects and the impression of even a theologian like Abdu'l Haq was that close ties remained.[136]

RELATION WITH HINDUS

Akbar decreed that Hindus who had been forced to convert to Islam could reconvert to Hinduism without facing the death penalty.[137]

Akbar in his days of tolerance was so well liked by Hindus that there are numerous references to him and his eulogies are sung in songs and religious hymns as well.[138]

Akbar practiced several Hindu customs. He celebrated Diwali. He allowed Brahman priests to tie jeweled strings round his wrists by way of blessing and, following his lead, many of the nobles took to wearing *rakhi* (protection charms).[139] He had renounced beef, and forbade the sale of all meats on certain days.[139] Also his royal queen-consort was a Hindu princess, Harkha Bai.

Even his son Jahangir and grandson Shahjahan maintained many of Akbar's concessions, such as the ban on cow slaughter, having only vegetarian dishes on certain days of the week, and drink only Ganges water.[140] Even as he was in the Punjab, 200 miles away from the Ganges, the water was sealed in large jars and transported to him. He referred to the Ganges water as the "water of immortality."[140]

It was rumored that each night a Brahman priest, suspended on a string cot pulled up to the window of Akbar's bedchamber, would captivate the emperor with tales of Hindu gods.[139]

RELATION WITH JAINS

Akbar regularly held discussions with Jain scholars and was also greatly impacted by some of their teachings. His first encounter with Jain rituals was when he saw a Jain shravika named Champa's procession after a six-month long fast. Impressed by her power and devotion, he invited her guru or spiritual teacher Acharya Hiravijaya Suri to Fatehpur Sikri. Acharya accepted the invitation and began his march towards the Mughal capital from Gujarat.[141]

Akbar was impressed by the scholastic qualities and character of the Acharya. He held several debates and discussions on religion and philosophy in his courts. Arguing with Jains, Akbar remained sceptical of their views on God and creation, and yet became convinced by their philosophy of non-violence and vegetarianism and ended up deploring the eating of all flesh.[142][*clarification needed*] Akbar also issued many imperial orders that were favorable for Jain interests, such as banning animal slaughter.[143] Jain authors also wrote about their experience at the Mughal court in Sanskrit texts that are still largely unknown to Mughal historians.[144]

The Indian Supreme Court has cited examples of co-existence of Jain and Mughal architecture, calling Akbar "the architect of modern India" and that "he had great respect" for Jainism. In 1592, 1584 and 1598, Akbar had declared "Amari Ghosana", which prohibited animal slaughter during Paryushan and Mahavir Jayanti. He removed the Jazia tax from Jain pilgrim places like Palitana.[145] Santichandra, disciple of Suri, was sent to the Emperor, who in turn left his disciples Bhanuchandra and Siddhichandra in the court. Akbar again invited Hiravijaya Suri's successor Vijayasena Suri in his court who visited him between 1593 to 1595.[*citation needed*]

Akbar's religious tolerance was not followed by his son Jahangir, who even threatened Akbar's former friend Bhanuchandra.[146]

HISTORICAL ACCOUNTS

Personality

Akbar's reign was chronicled extensively by his court historian Abul Fazal in the books *Akbarnama* and *Ain-i-akbari*. Other contemporary sources of Akbar's reign include the works of Badayuni, Shaikhzada Rashidi and Shaikh Ahmed Sirhindi.

Akbar was an artisan, warrior, artist, armourer, blacksmith, carpenter, emperor, general, inventor, animal trainer (reputedly keeping thousands of hunting cheetahs during his reign and training many himself), lacemaker, technologist and theologian.[147] Believed to be dyslexic, he was read to everyday and had a remarkable memory.[148]

Akbar was said to have been a wise emperor and a sound judge of character. His son and heir, Jahangir, wrote effusive praise of Akbar's character in his memoirs, and dozens of anecdotes to illustrate his virtues.[149] According to Jahangir, Akbar was "of the hue of wheat; his eyes and eyebrows were black and his complexion rather dark than fair". Antoni de Montserrat, the Catalan Jesuit who visited his court described him as follows:

"One could easily recognize even at first glance that he is King. He has broad shoulders, somewhat bandy legs well-suited for horsemanship, and a light brown complexion. He carries his head bent towards the right shoulder. His forehead is broad and open, his eyes so bright and flashing that they seem like a sea shimmering in the sunlight. His eyelashes are very long. His eyebrows are not strongly marked. His nose is straight and small though not insignificant. His nostrils are widely open as though in derision. Between the left nostril and the upper lip there is a mole. He shaves his beard but wears a moustache. He limps in his left leg though he has never received an injury there."[150]

Akbar was not tall but powerfully built and very agile. He was also noted for various acts of courage. One such incident occurred on his way back from Malwa to Agra when Akbar was 19 years of age. Akbar rode alone in advance of his escort and was confronted by a tigress who, along with her cubs, came out from the shrubbery across his path. When the tigress charged the emperor, he was alleged to have dispatched the animal with his sword in a solitary blow. His approaching attendants found the emperor standing quietly by the side of the dead animal.[151]

Abul Fazal, and even the hostile critic Badayuni, described him as having a commanding personality. He was notable for his command in battle, and, "like Alexander of Macedon, was always ready to risk his life, regardless of political consequences". He often plunged on his horse into the flooded river during the rainy seasons and safely crossed it. He rarely indulged in cruelty and is said to have been affectionate towards his relatives. He pardoned his brother Hakim, who was a repented rebel. But on rare occasions, he dealt cruelly with offenders, such as his maternal uncle Muazzam and his foster-brother Adham Khan, who was twice defenestrated for drawing Akbar's wrath.[152]

He is said to have been extremely moderate in his diet. *Ain-e-Akbari* mentions that during his travels and also while at home, Akbar drank water from the Ganges river, which he called 'the water of immortality'. Special people were stationed at Sorun and later Haridwar to dispatch water, in sealed jars, to wherever he was stationed.[153][better source needed] According to Jahangir's memoirs, he was fond of fruits and had little liking for meat, which he stopped eating in his later years. Akbar also once visited Vrindavan, the birthplace of Lord Krishna in the year 1570, and gave permission for four temples to be built by the Gaudiya Vaisnavas, which were Madana-mohana, Govindaji, Gopinatha and Jugal Kisore.

To defend his stance that speech arose from hearing, he carried out a language deprivation experiment, and had children raised in isolation, not allowed to be spoken to, and pointed out that as they grew older, they remained mute.[154]

HAGIOGRAPHY

During Akbar's reign, the ongoing process of inter-religious discourse and syncretism resulted in a series of religious attributions to him in terms of positions of assimilation, doubt or uncertainty, which he either assisted himself or left unchallenged.[155] Such hagiographical accounts of Akbar traversed a wide range of denominational and sectarian spaces, including several accounts by Parsis, Jains and Jesuit missionaries, apart from contemporary accounts by Brahminical and Muslim orthodoxy.[156] Existing sects and denominations, as well as various religious figures who represented popular worship felt they had a claim to him. The diversity of these accounts is attributed to the fact that his reign resulted in the formation of a flexible centralised state accompanied by personal authority and cultural heterogeneity.[155]

AKBARNĀMA, THE *BOOK OF AKBAR*

The Akbarnāma (Persian: نامہ اکبر), which literally means *Book of Akbar*, is an official biographical account of Akbar, the third Mughal Emperor (r. 1542–1605), written in Persian. It includes vivid and detailed descriptions of his life and times.[157]

The work was commissioned by Akbar, and written by Abul Fazl, one of the *Nine Jewels* (Hindi: Navaratnas) of Akbar's royal court. It is stated that the book took seven years to be completed and the original manuscripts contained a number of paintings supporting the texts, and all the paintings represented the Mughal school of painting, and work of masters of the imperial workshop, including Basawan, whose use of portraiture in its illustrations was an innovation in Indian art.[157]

DEATH

On 3 October 1605, Akbar fell ill with an attack of dysentery, from which he never recovered. He is believed to have died on or about 27 October 1605, after which his body was buried at a mausoleum in Sikandra, Agra.[158]

Seventy-six years later, in 1691, a group of austere Hindu rebels known as the Jats, rebelling against the Mughal Empire robbed the gold, silver and fine carpets within the tomb, desecrated Akbar's mausoleum.[159][160]

LEGACY

Akbar left behind a rich legacy both for the Mughal Empire as well as the Indian subcontinent in general. He firmly entrenched the authority of the Mughal empire in India and beyond, after it had been threatened by the Afghans during his father's reign,[161] establishing its military and diplomatic superiority.[162] During his reign, the nature of the state changed to a secular and liberal one, with emphasis on cultural integration. He also introduced several far-sighted social reforms, including prohibiting *sati*, legalising widow remarriage and raising the age of marriage. Folk tales revolving around him and Birbal, one of his *navratnas* are popular in India.

In *Bhavishya Purana*, a minor *Purana* that depicts the various Hindu holy days, includes a section devoted to the various dynasties which ruled India, having its oldest portion dated to 500 CE and newest to the 18th century, contains a special story focusing on Akbar, compared to the other Mughal rulers. The section called "Akbar Bahshaha Varnan" written in Sanskrit describes his birth as a "reincarnation" of a sage who self immolated himself on seeing the first Mughal ruler Babur described as the "cruel king of Mlecchas (Muslims)" and also that Akbar "was a miraculous child" and would not follow the previous "violent ways" of the Mughals.[163][164]

Citing Akbar's melding of the disparate 'fiefdoms' of India into the Mughal Empire as well as the lasting legacy of "pluralism and tolerance" that "underlies the values of the modern republic of India", Time magazine included his name in its list of top 25 world leaders.[165]

NOTES

1. ^ Jump up to: [a][b] Eraly, Abraham (2004). *The Mughal Throne: The Saga of India's Great Emperors*. Phoenix. pp. 115, 116. ISBN 9780753817582.
2. Jump up ^ "Akbar (Mughal emperor)". Encyclopedia Britannica Online. Retrieved 18 January 2013.
3. Jump up ^ "Google Images". Google.com.pk. Retrieved 2014-01-18.
4. Jump up ^ "Famous Birthdays on 15th October". Retrieved 21 October 2012.
5. Jump up ^ Eraly, Abraham (2000). *Emperors of the Peacock Throne : The Saga of the Great Mughals*. Penguin books. p. 189. ISBN 9780141001432.
6. ^ Jump up to: [a][b] "Akbar I". Encyclopaedia Iranica. 2011-07-29. Retrieved 2014-01-18.
7. Jump up ^ "Akbar I". Oxford Reference. 2012-02-17. Retrieved 2014-01-18.
8. Jump up ^ Umerkot's former Rajput ruler is dead
9. Jump up ^ Hoyland, J.S.; Banerjee S.N. (1996). *Commentary of Father Monserrate, S.J: On his journey to the court of Akbar, Asean Educational Services Published*. New Delhi: Asian Educational Services. p. 57. ISBN 81-206-0807-0.
10. Jump up ^ Banjerji, S.K. *Humayun Badshah*.
11. Jump up ^ Fazl, Abul. *Akbarnama Volume I*.
12. Jump up ^ Eraly, Abraham (2000). *Emperors of the Peacock Throne : the Saga of the Great Mughals*. Penguin books. p. 123. ISBN 9780141001432.
13. Jump up ^ Jahangir (1968). Henry Beveridge, ed. *The Tūzuk-i-Jahāngīrī: or, Memoirs of Jāhāngīr, Volumes 1-2*. Munshiram Manoharlal. p. 48.
14. Jump up ^ Ferishta, Mahomed Kasim (2013). *History of the Rise of the Mahomedan Power in India, Till the Year AD 1612*. Cambridge University Press. p. 169. ISBN 9781108055550.
15. Jump up ^ "Gurdas". Government of Punjab. Archived from the original on 27 May 2008. Retrieved 30 May 2008.[dead link]
16. Jump up ^ History Gurdaspur district website.
17. Jump up ^ Smith 2002, p. 337
18. ^ Jump up to: [a][b] Lal, Ruby (2005). *Domesticity and Power in the Early Mughal World*. Cambridge University Press. p. 140. ISBN 978-0521850223.

19. ^ Jump up to: [a][b] Kulke, Hermann (2004). *A history of India*. Routledge. p. 205. ISBN 978-0415329200.
20. **Jump up** ^ Schimmel, Annemarie (2004). *The Empire of the Great Mughals: History, Art, and Culture*. Reaktion Books. p. 88. ISBN 978-1861891853.
21. **Jump up** ^ Richards, John F. (1996). *The Mughal Empire*. Cambridge University Press. p. 288. ISBN 978-0521566032.
22. **Jump up** ^ Elgood, Robert (1995). *Firearms of the Islamic World*. I.B.Tauris. p. 135. ISBN 978-1850439639.
23. **Jump up** ^ Gommans, Jos (2002). *Mughal Warfare: Indian Frontiers and High Roads to Empire, 1500-1700*. Routledge. p. 134. ISBN 978-0415239882.
24. ^ Jump up to: [a][b][c][d][e] Eraly, Abraham (2000). *Emperors of the Peacock Throne: The Saga of the Great Mughals*. Penguin Books India. pp. 118–124. ISBN 978-0141001432.
25. **Jump up** ^ Majumdar 1984, pp. 104–105
26. **Jump up** ^ Chandra 2007, pp. 226–227
27. ^ Jump up to: [a][b] Chandra 2007, p. 227
28. ^ Jump up to: [a][b][c][d][e][f][g] Richards, John F. (1996). *The Mughal Empire*. Cambridge University Press. pp. 9–13. ISBN 978-0521566032.
29. ^ Jump up to: [a][b][c][d][e][f][g][h][i][j][k] Richards, John F. (1996). *The Mughal Empire*. Cambridge University Press. pp. 14–15. ISBN 978-0521566032.
30. **Jump up** ^ Smith 2002, p. 339
31. **Jump up** ^ Chandra 2007, p. 228
32. ^ Jump up to: [a][b][c][d][e][f][g][h][i][j][k] Eraly, Abraham (2000). *Emperors of the Peacock Throne: The Saga of the Great Mughals*. Penguin Books India. pp. 140–141. ISBN 978-0141001432.
33. ^ Jump up to: [a][b] Richards, John F. (1996). *The Mughal Empire*. Cambridge University Press. pp. 17–21. ISBN 978-0521566032.
34. ^ Jump up to: [a][b][c][d][e][f][g] Chandra, Satish (2005). *Medieval India: From Sultanat to the Mughals Part - II*. Har-Anand Publications. pp. 105–106. ISBN 978-8124110669.
35. ^ Jump up to: [a][b] Chandra 2007, p. 231
36. **Jump up** ^ Smith 2002, p. 342
37. **Jump up** ^ Chandra, Dr. Satish (2001). *Medieval India: From Sultanat to the Mughals*. Har Anand Publications. p. 107. ISBN 81-241-0522-7.
38. **Jump up** ^ Payne, Tod (1994). *Tod's Annals of Rajasthan: The Annals of Mewar*. Asian Educational Services. p. 71. ISBN 81-206-0350-8.
39. **Jump up** ^ Eraly, Abraham (2007). *The Mughal World*. Penguin Books India. p. 11. ISBN 978-0141001432.

40.   ^ Jump up to: [a b c d e f g h i j k l m n] Eraly, Abraham (2000). *Emperors of the Peacock Throne: The Saga of the Great Mughals*. Penguin Books India. pp. 143–147. ISBN 978-0141001432.

41.   **Jump up** ^ Hastings, James (2003). *Encyclopedia of Religion and Ethics Part 10*. Kessinger Publishing. ISBN 0-7661-3682-5.

42.   **Jump up** ^ Chandra 2007, p. 232

43.   ^ Jump up to: [a b] Richards, John F. (1996). *The Mughal Empire*. Cambridge University Press. p. 32. ISBN 978-0521566032.

44.   ^ Jump up to: [a b c d e f g h i j k l m] Eraly, Abraham (2000). *Emperors of the Peacock Throne: The Saga of the Great Mughals*. Penguin Books India. pp. 148–154. ISBN 978-0141001432.

45.   **Jump up** ^ Pletcher, Kenneth (2010). *Emperors of the Peacock Throne: The Saga of the Great Mughals*. The Rosen Publishing Group. p. 170. ISBN 978-1615302017.

46.   ^ Jump up to: [a b c] "The Age of Akbar". columbia.edu. Retrieved 31 May 2013.

47.   ^ Jump up to: [a b c d e f] Dani, Ahmad Hasan Dani; Chahryar Adle; Irfan Habib (2002). *History of Civilizations of Central Asia: Development in Contrast: From the Sixteenth to the Mid-Nineteenth Century*. UNESCO. pp. 276–277. ISBN 978-9231027192.

48.   ^ Jump up to: [a b c d e f g h i j k] Richards, John F. (1996). *The Mughal Empire*. Cambridge University Press. pp. 49–51. ISBN 978-0521566032.

49.   **Jump up** ^ Markovitz, Claude (2002). *A History of Modern India: 1480 - 1950*. Anthem Press. p. 93. ISBN 978-1843310044.

50.   ^ Jump up to: [a b c d e f g h i j k] Eraly, Abraham (2000). *Emperors of the Peacock Throne: The Saga of the Great Mughals*. Penguin Books India. pp. 156–157. ISBN 978-0141001432.

51.   ^ Jump up to: [a b c d] Mehta, J.L. (2000). *Advanced Study In The History Of Medieval India*. Sterling Publishers. p. 258. ISBN 978-8120710153.

52.   **Jump up** ^ Houtsma, M.T. (1993). *E. J. Brill's First Encyclopaedia of Islam, 1913-1936, Volume 4*. BRILL. p. 711. ISBN 978-9004097964.

53.   ^ Jump up to: [a b c d] Floor, Willem; Edmund Herzig (2012). *Iran and the World in the Safavid Age*. I.B.Tauris. p. 136. ISBN 978-1850439301.

54.   **Jump up** ^ Chandra 2007, p. 233

55.   ^ Jump up to: [a b] Chandra 2007, p. 234

56.   ^ Jump up to: [a b] Chandra 2007, p. 236

57.   **Jump up** ^ Moosvi 2008, p. 160

58. ^ Jump up to: *a b* Chandra 2007, p. 235
59. **Jump up** ^ Moosvi 2008, pp. 164–165
60. **Jump up** ^ Moosvi 2008, p. 165
61. **Jump up** ^ Smith 2002, p. 359
62. ^ Jump up to: *a b* Chandra 2007, p. 238
63. **Jump up** ^ Chandra 2007, p. 237
64. **Jump up** ^ Petersen, A. (1996). *Dictionary of Islamic Architecture*. New York: Routledge.
65. **Jump up** ^ "Economic and Social Developments under the Mughals". columbia.edu. Retrieved 30 May 2013.
66. ^ Jump up to: *a b c* Levi, S. C. (2002). *The Indian Diaspora in Central Asia and Its Trade: 1550 - 1900*. BRILL. p. 39. ISBN 978-9004123205.
67. ^ Jump up to: *a b c d* Chandra 2007, p. 243
68. ^ Jump up to: *a b* Sarkar 1984, p. 37
69. **Jump up** ^ Atul Sethi (24 June 2007). "'Trade, not invasion brought Islam to India'". The Times of India. Retrieved 2008-02-15.
70. ^ Jump up to: *a b* Ashley D'Mello (2005-12-10). "Fact, myth blend in re-look at Akbar-Jodha Bai". The Times of India. Retrieved 2008-02-15.
71. **Jump up** ^ Sarkar 1984, p. 36
72. **Jump up** ^ Chandra 2007, pp. 242–243
73. **Jump up** ^ Nath 1982, p. 52
74. **Jump up** ^ Alam, Muzaffar; Subrahmanyam, Sanjay (1998). *The Mughal State, 1526-1750*. Oxford University Press. p. 177. ISBN 978-0-19-563905-6.
75. **Jump up** ^ Sarkar 1984, pp. 38–40
76. **Jump up** ^ Sarkar 1984, p. 38
77. **Jump up** ^ Maryam Juzer Kherulla (12 October 2002). "Profile: Tansen — the mesmerizing maestro". Dawn (newspaper). Retrieved 2 October 2007.[*dead link*]
78. **Jump up** ^ India Divided, By Rajendra Prasad, pg. 63
79. **Jump up** ^ A History of Hindi Literature, By F. E. Keay, pg. 36
80. **Jump up** ^ Newton, Arthur Percival. *"The Cambridge history of the British Empire, Volume 2'&#39*. Books.google.com. p. 14. Retrieved 2014-01-18.
81. **Jump up** ^ Habib 1997, p. 256
82. **Jump up** ^ Habib 1997, pp. 256–257
83. **Jump up** ^ Habib 1997, p. 259
84. **Jump up** ^ Frances Pritchett. "XVI. Mughal Administration". Columbia.edu. Retrieved 2014-01-18.
85. **Jump up** ^ Frances Pritchett. "XIX. A Century of Political Decline: 1707-1803". Columbia.edu. Retrieved 2014-01-18.
86. **Jump up** ^ Habib 1997, p. 260

87.   **Jump up** ^ Will Durant (7 June 2011). *Our Oriental Heritage: The Story of Civilization*. Simon and Schuster. pp. 738–. ISBN 978-1-4516-4668-9. Retrieved 27 August 2012.

88.   **Jump up** ^ Frances Pritchett. "XII. Religion at Akbar's Court". Columbia.edu. Retrieved 2014-01-18.

89.   **Jump up** ^ Dr Farhan Ahmad Nizami (2014-01-01). "Six Ottoman Documents On Mughal-Ottoman Relations During The Reign Of Akbar". Jis.oxfordjournals.org. Retrieved 2014-01-18.

90.   **Jump up** ^ "Book Reviews : NAIMUR RAHMAN FAROOQI, Mughal-Ottoman Relations: A Study of the Political and Diplomatic Relations between Mughal India and the Ottoman Empire, 1556-1748, Delhi". ler.sagepub.com. 1994-06-01. Retrieved 2014-01-18.

91.   **Jump up** ^ *Mughal-Ottoman relations: a study of political & diplomatic relations ... - Naimur Rahman Farooqi - Google Boeken*. Books.google.com. Retrieved 2014-01-18.

92.   **Jump up** ^ Moosvi 2008, p. 246

93.   **Jump up** ^ Ottoman court chroniclers (1578). *Muhimme Defterleri, Vol. 32 f 292 firman 740, Shaban 986.*

94.   **Jump up** ^ Khan, Iqtidar Alam (1999). *Akbar and his age*. Northern Book Centre. p. 218. ISBN 978-81-7211-108-3.

95.   ^ Jump up to: [a][b] *The Ottoman Empire And the World Around It - Suraiya Faroqhi*. Google Books.pk. Retrieved 2012-06-12.

96.   **Jump up** ^ *Mughal-Ottoman relations: a study of political & diplomatic relations ... - Naimur Rahman Farooqi - Google Boeken*. Books.google.com. Retrieved 2014-01-18.

97.   **Jump up** ^ *The Ottoman Empire And the World Around It - Suraiya Faroqhi*. Google Books.pk. 2006-03-03. ISBN 9781845111229. Retrieved 2012-06-12.

98.   **Jump up** ^ *Mughal-Ottoman relations: a study of political & diplomatic relations ... - Naimur Rahman Farooqi - Google Boeken*. Books.google.com. Retrieved 2014-01-18.

99.   **Jump up** ^ Majumdar 1984, p. 158

100. **Jump up** ^ Ottoman court chroniclers (1588). *Muhimme Defterleri, Vol. 62 f 205 firman 457, Avail Rabiulavval 996.*

101. **Jump up** ^ Ali 2006, p. 94

102. ^ Jump up to: [a][b] Majumdar 1984, p. 153

103. **Jump up** ^ Ali 2006, pp. 327–328

104. **Jump up** ^ Majumdar 1984, p. 154

105. **Jump up** ^ Majumdar 1984, pp. 154–155

106. **Jump up** ^ Majumdar 1984, pp. 153–154

107. **Jump up** ^ Ali 2006, p. 327

108.   **Jump up** ^ Majumdar 1984, p. 155
109.   **Jump up** ^ VA Smith (1919). *Akbar the Great Moghul.* Oxford. p. 292.
110.   **Jump up** ^ *Asia in the Making of Europe, Volume III: A Century of Advance. Book 1* by Donald F. Lach,Edwin J. Van Kley p.393 [1]
111.   **Jump up** ^ Habib 1997, p. 80
112.   ^ Jump up to: *a b c* Chandra 2007, p. 253
113.   **Jump up** ^ Chandra 2007, p. 252
114.   **Jump up** ^ Hasan 2007, p. 72
115.   ^ Jump up to: *a b* Habib 1997, p. 81
116.   **Jump up** ^ Habib 1997, p. 85
117.   ^ Jump up to: *a b c* Habib 1997, p. 86
118.   **Jump up** ^ Ali 2006, pp. 165–166
119.   ^ Jump up to: *a b c* Chandra 2007, p. 254
120.   **Jump up** ^ Ali 2006, p. 159
121.   **Jump up** ^ Hasan 2007, p. 79
122.   **Jump up** ^ Hasan 2007, pp. 82–83
123.   **Jump up** ^ The Turks in India by G.H. Keene
124.   **Jump up** ^ Chandra 2007, p. 255
125.   **Jump up** ^ Chandra 2007, p. 256
126.   **Jump up** ^ "Din-i Ilahi — Britannica Online Encyclopedia". Britannica.com. Retrieved 18 July 2009.
127.   **Jump up** ^ Sharma, Sri Ram (1988). *The Religious Policy of the Mughal Emperors.* Munshiram Manoharlal Publishers. p. 42. ISBN 81-215-0395-7.
128.   **Jump up** ^ Smith 2002, p. 348
129.   **Jump up** ^ Roy Choudhury, Makhan Lal (1941). *The Din-i-Ilahi, or, The religion of Akbar* (3rd ed.). New Delhi: Oriental Reprint (published 1985, 1997). ISBN 81-215-0777-4Check date values in: |publicationdate= (help)
130.   **Jump up** ^ Majumdar 1984, p. 138
131.   **Jump up** ^ Koka,Aziz (1594). *King's College Collection, MS 194.* This letter is preserved in Cambridge University Library. p. ff.5b-8b.
132.   **Jump up** ^ Conder, Josiah (1828). *The Modern Traveller: a popular description.* R.H.Tims. p. 282.
133.   **Jump up** ^ Deefholts, Margaret; Deefholts, Glenn; Acharya, Quentine (2006). *The Way We Were: Anglo-Indian Cronicles.* Calcutta Tiljallah Relief Inc. p. 87. ISBN 0-9754639-3-4.
134.   **Jump up** ^ Ali 2006, pp. 163–164
135.   **Jump up** ^ Ali 2006, p. 164
136.   **Jump up** ^ Habib 1997, p. 96
137.   **Jump up** ^ P. 187 *Day of Empire: How Hyperpowers Rise to Global Dominance--and Why They Fall* By Amy Chua
138.   **Jump up** ^ P. 126 *Day of Empire: How Hyperpowers Rise to Global Dominance--and Why They Fall* By Amy Chua

139. ^ Jump up to: [a] [b] [c] P. 30 *Curry: A Tale of Cooks and Conquerors* By Lizzie Collingham

140. ^ Jump up to: [a] [b] P. 31 *Curry: A Tale of Cooks and Conquerors* By Lizzie Collingham

141. **Jump up** ^ Sanghmitra. *Jain Dharma ke Prabhavak Acharya*. Jain Vishwa Bharati, Ladnu.

142. **Jump up** ^ Sen, Amartya (2005). "13". *The Argumentative Indian*. Allen Lane. ISBN 0-7139-9687-0.

143. **Jump up** ^ Truschke, Audrey. "Jains and the Mughals". JAINpedia.[dead link]

144. **Jump up** ^ Truschke, Audrey. "Setting the Record Wrong: A Sanskrit Vision of Mughal Conquests".

145. **Jump up** ^ "Ahmedabad turned Akbar veggie". The Times of India. 23 November 2009. Retrieved 23 November 2009.

146. **Jump up** ^ P. 137, *Poetry of Kings: The Classical Hindi Literature of Mughal India* by Allison Busch

147. **Jump up** ^ Habib, Irfan (1992). "Akbar and Technology". *Social Scientist* 20 (9–10): 3–15. doi:10.2307/3517712.

148. **Jump up** ^ John F. Richards, *The Mughal Empire*, (Cambridge University Press, 1995), 35.

149. **Jump up** ^ Jahangir (1600s). *Tuzk-e-Jahangiri (Memoirs of Jahangir)*.

150. **Jump up** ^ [2]"Portraits of Akbar, the Great Mughal" by Tancred Borenius The Burlington Magazine for Connoisseurs Vol. 82, No. 480 (Mar., 1943), pp. 54+67-68

151. **Jump up** ^ Garbe, Richard von (1909). *Akbar, Emperor of India*. Chicago-The Open Court Publishing Company.

152. **Jump up** ^ John F. Richards, *The Mughal Empire*, (Cambridge University Press, 1995), 15.

153. **Jump up** ^ Hardwar Ain-e-Akbari, by Abul Fazl 'Allami, Volume I, A'I'N 22. The A'bda'r Kha'nah. P 55. Translated from the original Persian, by Heinrich Blochmann and Colonel Henry Sullivan Jarrett, Asiatic society of Bengal. Calcutta, 1873 – 1907.

154. **Jump up** ^ "1200—1750". University of Hamburg. Retrieved 30 May 2008.

155. ^ Jump up to: [a] [b] Sangari 2007, p. 497

156. **Jump up** ^ Sangari 2007, p. 475

157. ^ Jump up to: [a] [b] Illustration from the Akbarnama: History of Akbar Art Institute of Chicago

158. **Jump up** ^ Majumdar 1984, pp. 168–169

159. **Jump up** ^ "Aurangzeb". New World Encyclopedia. Retrieved 2014-01-18.

160. **Jump up** ^ Asher, Catherine B (1992-09-24). "Architecture of Mughal India". ISBN 9780521267281.

161. **Jump up** ^ Habib 1997, p. 79

162. **Jump up** ^ Majumdar 1984, p. 170

163.   **Jump up** ^ Meenakshi Khanna (2007). *Cultural History Of Medieval India*. Berghahn Books. pp. 34–35. ISBN 978-81-87358-30-5. Retrieved 30 June 2013.
164.   **Jump up** ^ *The Imperial and Asiatic Quarterly Review and Oriental and Colonial Record*. Oriental Institute. 1900. pp. 158–161. Retrieved 29 June 2013.
165.   **Jump up** ^ Tharoor, Ishaan (4 February 2011). "Top 25 Political Icons:Akbar the Great". Time magazine.

FURTHER READING

Abu'l-Fazl ibn Mubarak *Akbar-namah* Edited with commentary by Muhammad Sadiq Ali (Kanpur-Lucknow: Nawal Kishore) 1881–3 Three Vols. (Persian)

Abu al-Fazl ibn Mubarak *Akbarnamah* Edited by Maulavi Abd al-Rahim. Bibliotheca Indica Series (Calcutta: Asiatic Society of Bengal) 1877–1887 Three Vols. (Persian)

Henry Beveridge (Trans.) *The Akbarnama of Ab-ul-Fazl* Bibliotheca Indica Series (Calcutta: Asiatic Society of Bengal) 1897 Three Vols.

Haji Muhammad 'Arif Qandahari *Tarikh-i-Akbari (Better known as Tarikh-i-Qandahari)* edited & Annotated by Haji Mu'in'd-Din Nadwi, Dr. Azhar 'Ali Dihlawi & Imtiyaz 'Ali 'Arshi (Rampur Raza Library) 1962 (Persian)

Martí Escayol, Maria Antònia. "Antoni de Montserrat in the Mughal Garden of good government European construction of Indian nature", *Word, Image, Text: Studies in Literary and Visual Culture*, ed. Shormistha Panja et al., Orient Blackswan, New Delhi, 2009. ISBN 978-81-250-3735-4

Satyananda Giri, *Akbar*, Trafford Publishing, 2009, ISBN 978-1-4269-1561-1

Augustus, Frederick; (tr. by Annette Susannah Beveridge) (1890). *The Emperor Akbar, a contribution towards the history of India in the 16th century (Vol. 1)*. Thacker, Spink and Co., Calcutta.

Augustus, Frederick; (tr. by Annette Susannah Beveridge) (1890). Gustav von Buchwald, ed. *The Emperor Akbar, a contribution towards the history of India in the 16th century (Vol. 2)*. Thacker, Spink and Co., Calcutta.

Malleson, Colonel G. B. (1899). *Akbar And The Rise Of The Mughal Empire*. Rulers of India series. Oxford at the Clarendon Press.

Garbe, Dr. Richard von (1909). *Akbar - Emperor of India. A Picture of Life and Customs from the Sixteenth Century*. The Opencourt Publishing Company, Chicago.

- o *Akbar, Emperor of India* by Richard von Garbe 1857-1927 - (ebook)

The Adventures of Akbar by Flora Annie Steel, 1847-1929 -(ebook)

Smith, Vincent Arthur (1917). *Akbar the Great Mogul, 1542-1605*. Oxford at The Clarendon Press.

Havell, E. B. (1918). *The History of Aryan Rule In India from the earliest times to the death of Akbar*. Frederick A. Stokes Co., New York.

Moreland, W. H. (1920). *India at the death of Akbar: An economic study*. Macmillan & Co., London.

Monserrate, Father Antonio (1922). *The commentary of Father Monserrate, S.J., on his journey to the court of Akbar*. Oxford University Press

www.ingramcontent.com/pod-product-compliance
Lightning Source LLC
Chambersburg PA
CBHW030346030726
47499CB00003B/921